LIFE CYCLE OF A LIE

life cycle of a LIE

sylvia olsen

sononis
PRESS

LIBRARY AND ARCHIVES CANADA CATALOGUING IN PUBLICATION

Olsen, Sylvia, 1955–, author
Life cycle of a lie / Sylvia Olsen.

Issued in print and electronic formats.
ISBN 978-1-55039-233-3 (pbk.)–ISBN 978-1-55039-238-8 (ebook)

I. Title.
PS8579.L728L53 2014 jC813'.6 C2014-906028-9 C2014-906029-7

Sono Nis Press most gratefully acknowledges support for our publishing program provided by the Government of Canada through the Canada Book Fund and the Canada Council for the Arts, and by the Province of British Columbia through the British Columbia Arts Council and the Book Publishing Tax Credit, Ministry of Provincial Revenue.

Edited by Barbara Pulling and Nikki Tate
Copy edited by Audrey McClellan
Proofread by Dawn Loewen
Cover and interior design by Frances Hunter

Published by
SONO NIS PRESS
Box 160
Winlaw, BC V0G 2J0
1-800-370-5228

Distributed in the U.S. by
ORCA BOOK PUBLISHERS
Box 468
Custer, WA 98240-0468
1-800-210-5277

books@sononis.com
www.sononis.com

Printed and bound in Canada by Houghton Boston Printing.
Printed on acid-free paper that is forest friendly (100% post-consumer recycled paper) and has been processed chlorine free.

Uncovering a lie can uncover a whole lot more

than that—it can uncover who we really are.

First Day of School

Vik

"Hey! I'm Vik. Welcome."

"I'm Jona. Pull up a stump!"

I laughed, because he was sitting on the only stump outside Forestview Secondary School.

"You're new here, right?" I asked, though I knew the answer already.

He nodded.

"Why don't we wait inside?" I said, tipping my head toward the front doors. "The last bus isn't here yet, so the principal won't start the opening ceremony on time. And before long this mist is going to turn into rain."

He jumped off the stump.

"Where are you from?"

"Vancouver," he said. "Nice nail polish. Aubergine."

I smiled. *Aubergine?* What kind of a guy was this?

"Eggplant," he said. "It's one of my favourite colours. To think they used to just call it purple."

"Glad you like it. And thanks for the explanation. Now I don't have to Google 'aubergine' to see what it means."

He laughed, and his long black ponytail slipped from side to side across his back. He had to be the only boy in Carterton who would even notice a girl's nail polish, never mind say something about the colour. How was he going to survive? He needed a friend to show him the ropes, or he was going to get chewed up and spit out so fast he wouldn't know what hit him.

"C'mon, I'll take you for the grand tour. For what it's worth. Forestview Secondary. Hah! The view of the forest must have been a lot better before they clear-cut our hills. Now it looks like patchwork."

"I noticed."

We headed down the hall past pockets of kids huddled along the way. Everyone gawked. It was more than his purple leather high-tops and pale green cardigan. It was the way Jona moved, like a dancer. A few girls snapped cell photos of him, as if they were looking at an exotic animal.

"Don't mind them," I said. "New kids are a rare species in this school. Everyone moves out of Carterton. No one moves in."

When we reached the cafeteria, the place was crowded. First Nations kids sat at tables on one side, and white kids on the other, which was a perfect description of the configuration of Forestview—and the town of Carterton, for that matter.

I sat in a chair near a First Nations table. "How about we sit down?"

His colouring made him look First Nations, but I was thinking that maybe he was Mexican or Brazilian or from some tropical country.

Jona gave the kids at the table a nod, and a few of the guys mumbled "bro" under their breath. Suddenly I got that possessive grade school thing, like, Jona was my friend first. He was different from everybody else around here, and I wanted part of him. It was like the first time I went to Vancouver, to the Science Centre on a field trip, and I tasted chocolate with salt.

It made all the other chocolate I'd ever eaten seem drab and uninteresting. He was the most exciting boy I'd ever seen in real life. Except Linc, of course.

"You're going to love my boyfriend, Linc. He'll be here on the bus. And just so you know—late around here doesn't mean much. Everything is late. It's enough to make you crazy."

"No worries. Time is just a construction, other than the fact that the earth goes around the sun and the seasons rotate in cycles. The rest of it we make up."

I thought, *Oh my God, I have never heard a guy talk like that.*

I threw my binder on the table.

"Whoa," Jona said, looking at it. "Don't tell me you are in that much distress."

It took me a moment to realize he was referring to the SOS collage I had made all over the cover.

He grinned. "Save Our Souls? Save Our Selves?"

I shook my head and wondered how to respond. I mean, what urban chic kid from Vancouver was going to care about cleaning up streams? But no genius comment came to mind, so I said, "It's a club. We're cleaning up streams so the salmon can come back."

I figured I was going to have to explain about spawning and how the clear-cuts had made that impossible, and maybe even what clear-cuts were, but before I could go on he unzipped his backpack and pulled out a book.

"Do you know this book? It's old, but amazing!"

I took the book and looked from the cover back to Jona's concerned expression. *Stein: The Way of the River.* "Have you read this?" I asked.

"No. But it was one of my latest finds at the second-hand bookstore in Vancouver, and I plan to read it. Until then I carry it around in case I meet someone who cleans up streams. You know, to make a good impression."

I punched him lightly in the shoulder. "You're pretty funny for a city boy." What the hell was I doing? I couldn't go around laughing and teasing a guy I didn't even know. "But you're right. I'm impressed.

"Maybe Save Our Selves would be a good name, but it really stands for Save Our Streams. There are seven of us on the committee. We've been working up on Statluk Mountain for the past year. We get rid of plants that are invasive species, drag snags out of the stream, and rebuild the banks. A biologist is helping us get it right. He figures another year or so and salmon will find their way back up to spawn."

"No way," he said. "I can't believe this. My first day of school and I've met someone interested in cleaning up the environment." He continued, talking fast, "I'd love to be part of your group. In Vancouver I was an armchair specialist. You know, somebody who's read all the books and can talk a good talk. But now that I'm here"—he waved his arm toward the emergency exit—"I'd love to go up a real mountain and work on a real stream."

"Don't worry. You will have your wish," I said.

Wow, he *can't believe it,* I thought. I was getting my wish as well—a new guy who wanted to join the committee. "Our first meeting this fall is in a month—the first Friday in October. And the next day we're going up to replant around the banks of the stream."

I flipped through the book and imagined how beautiful Statluk would have been if George Carter hadn't ripped it to shreds and left it looking like Armageddon.

Jona leaned over and pointed at a photo of the biggest trees I had ever seen. "The Stein Valley is an old-growth forest just a few hours north of Vancouver. A bunch of people fought the logging companies thirty years ago and now it's a park. Someday I'm going up there."

"I'd love to see it," I said. "Can I borrow this?"

"Keep it as long as you like. I collect books from secondhand bookstores. I've got a whole bunch of them—they cost like a buck each."

I was tucking the book into my binder when the doors to the cafeteria flew open. Linc caught my eye and threw me a huge smile. He strode across the room, high-fiving a few people sitting at the tables.

He stretched his arms out and I fell into his embrace. "Mmmmm…" Intoxicating. After a couple of seconds I pulled away.

"You've got to meet Jona," I said. I turned to Jona. "You've got to meet Linc."

They shook hands and clapped each other on the back. Linc was his usual gorgeous self, but Jona looked awkward, like maybe he was shy with guys or something.

"Jonas?" Linc said, looking super interested. "Did Vik say your name is Jonas?"

"Jona. You don't need the s."

"You from…?"

"Vancouver. Also without an s."

Linc laughed. "Welcome to our humble little town. It's not much compared to the big city. But hey, there's a party at the beach after supper if you want to come."

"Yeah," Jona said, without taking his eyes off Linc. "For sure."

I thought, *Yeah, right, Linc, humble little town. Little hick town, more like.* But maybe if more people like Jona moved to Carterton, I wouldn't be in such a hurry to get out of the place.

Jona

I paced around the porch, trying to decide what to do. A beach party after the first day of school sounded like an overdose of strangers, but staying home didn't seem like a great idea either. So I headed down the road toward the beach. I figured as long as Vik and Linc were there, I could handle a crowd. In a way the day had been better than I had expected. With an invitation to join an environmental group *and* a party already, the place couldn't be all bad.

Moving to Carterton hadn't been my choice. I didn't even know it existed until Aunt Lonnie told Mom and me it was where we were going to live. Looking at it one way—a two-bedroom trailer in the forest, only a short walk from the beach, in a small town only forty-five minutes from a slightly bigger town, Simpson Mills, that was only half a day from Victoria—the place sounded like prime real estate. The trailer was a bit of a dump, but I didn't mind. It was a hell of a lot better than our tenth-floor apartment in Vancouver's east side.

But looking at it another way, the move didn't seem so good. There was nothing like George's Basement in Carterton. There was probably nothing like George's anywhere, though. Anytime, day or night, I could bring my guitar and jam down under the old house on Main Street. There was always a different selection of musicians to jam with and try out new lyrics.

George's was the musicians' mecca on the east side. The other problem with Carterton: as far as I could tell, the place didn't have a library. So other than my second-hand book collection, there were no books. I didn't know how I was going to live without the fourth floor in the library, where I spent half my life reading.

As I walked toward the party, I looked at the giant cedar trees, the fern-covered forest floor, the moss that ballooned over the rocks, and the eagles that were soaring in circles, high in the grey sky over my head, and I thought these might be pretty good substitutes for some of the things I'd miss about Vancouver. I listened to the surf pounding the beach. It was like this place had a heartbeat that didn't quit. I started to hum, and soon some words popped into my head.

I found a place,
a space under the side of the moon
trace its superhero face, retrace...

Then the words lined up differently...

The moon's place, retrace, its superhero face
The space is maniacal, hysterical, heretical
a Greek god of miracles.

I was thinking about Linc as I walked, how his face and body looked like they were chiselled out of stone. Michelangelo's *David*. I quickened my pace to cool down the burn in my groin, and then I was running.

"Hey, you the guy Vik was telling me about?"

The voice was coming from a group of kids sitting on logs and stumps in a circle around a fire. It was getting dark by now, so I couldn't see who was talking. Then a girl, no bigger than a little kid, stood up, jumped over a log, and headed toward me.

"I'm talking to you. I'm Ruby, Linc's cousin. Truth is I've got lots of cousins around here, but Linc is like my brother. His mom, Sandy, she's my mom's sister, but she's like my mom too. My mom and I live next door to them, over on the reserve. But I guess you could say I almost live at Linc's place. I'm in grade eleven,and I'm Vik's best friend. How come you moved to Carterton?"

I stepped back and put my hands up.

The girl laughed. "Sorry," she said. "Everyone says I talk too much. I hear you're from Vancouver. It'll take some getting used to, living around here. We're roasting wieners. You hungry?"

Ruby was so friendly I couldn't help relaxing a bit.

"No, I'm fine."

"Now, tell me about you," she said.

"What do you want to know?"

"Everything."

"I'm like you. An only kid. But I don't have any cousins. I've got one aunt in Toronto, no grandparents. It's just Mom and me. That's it."

"Holy, that's crazy small. But that can't be it. Aren't you First Nations? You must have more people in your family than that."

"Yeah, I am. And yeah, I do. I guess." What a stupid answer. "Let me put it this way: my dad was a Mohawk, so I guess I've got family somewhere."

I was glad when a couple of vans drove up and interrupted our conversation. A dozen more people poured out onto the beach. Ruby shone her phone flashlight on a guy dragging a cooler. "Looks like you're going to party hearty tonight."

He smirked and said, "Cousin," then gave her a high-five. I could see him looking at me in the light cast by the fire.

"This is Jona," Ruby said. She poked her finger into my chest. "And this is Billy. He's one of the things around here that will take some getting used to."

It was lucky Billy cracked a smile, because he had a fierce look on his face that was starting to worry me.

"Hey, there's Linc and Vik." Ruby started to head in their direction and then stopped. "Oops, private time. Looks like something heavy going on." She called across the fire, "Hi guys."

Linc and Vik waved at her, then nodded at me. Linc was sitting on a log and Vik was on the sand in front of him. He leaned over and began to massage her shoulders.

Something was up. She didn't look like the sparkly girl I'd met in the morning.

Ruby sighed. "Oh, God. It looks like Bert's been at her again."

"Huh?"

"Vik's dad. He never quits giving her a hard time. She'll be fine, though. There's nothing Linc's massages can't heal."

I watched Vik rolling her shoulders in pleasure. "I see what you mean."

"Hey, you, new boy." A girl with very long legs came our way. "You want a beer?"

"No, thanks."

The girl held a can up to my lips. "You want *my* beer?"

I didn't want to say no again and look like a loser, so I said, "Sure."

She poured some beer into my mouth and laughed as it dribbled down my chin. I hated the taste, as always, but I tried not to grimace.

“His name is Jona, Ashley,” Ruby said. “In case you were wondering.”

“I’m going to get another beer,” Ashley said, handing me the can. She made sure I was watching her as she sauntered over, took another can from the cooler, and straddled Billy.

Someone had cranked up some tunes and was playing country music. Maggie Little. “*Shakin’ it, shakin’ it. I’m glowing in the dark, I’m dancing in the park.*” There hadn’t been much country music at George’s, but out here on the beach it seemed to fit in.

Ruby brought over a bag of chips. “Pull up a log,” she said, and we sat down. She passed me the chips. “Want some?”

“Thanks.”

“Hey, bro, when is it my turn?” Billy shouted to Linc.

Vik and Linc were just talking by then. She shouted back, “You can have him. I’m done with him.”

Billy lay face down on the sand. Linc kneeled beside him. Firelight flickered and glinted off his flexing biceps as he rubbed Billy’s shoulders.

“Linc’s our hands-on guy,” Ruby said when she saw me watching. “He wants to be a chiropractor or something touchy like that. Line up and you’ll get a turn.”

Just the thought of it made me tremble. I took another swig of beer, held my breath, and gulped. It still tasted like shit, but it calmed me down.

Vik and Ashley had started dancing together. The beat was hardcore, but my own words and rhythms started to flow again in my head…

the superhero
man on the go

dancing with the devil's angels
in heaven's smooth moving grooving hell
tell me how to glow bro

Ruby grabbed my hand and pulled me up to join the dancers.

"Whoa," I said. "Country music? Dancing? I don't know." But she wouldn't take no for an answer so I followed her.

I tried to focus, but I couldn't resist glancing over at Linc and Billy. Linc's movements were like thick liquid, warming Billy up until he was totally blissed out.

When Linc was finished, he got up and started dancing too.

"Jona's in line for a massage," Ruby yelled.

"Really?" Linc shouted over the music. "You want a turn?"

"No, no, don't worry about it." My knees wobbled, and I started to feel so light-headed I stumbled. He reached out and gripped my shoulders.

"No problem. I'm practising my trade." His mouth was close to my ear so I could hear. "One day I'll be a professional—physiotherapist or something like that."

"Feels like you've got magic hands."

I turned around and he kept massaging my shoulders from behind until Vik came over and moved his hands from my back.

"We have to go," she said. "I don't know about the rest of you, but I'm going to be at school tomorrow."

"Yeah, you're right," I said. "I just intended to stay a little while."

She smiled at me. "It's good to see you again."

"You need a ride?" Linc asked.

"No, thanks. I like the walk."

Ruby left with them, and most of the others started packing up.

Vik

I loved the sound of my phone. Every time it rang, I got a rush of the smell of Linc after a soccer game. My skin would tingle as if I was flooded with a cool wave. It might sound weird, but the jingle was like one of those psychological triggers. Like when a song reminds you of the place you first heard it. Only, for me, the ringtone reminded me of Linc's sweaty smell.

I guess it was love at first scent with me and Linc. Corny, maybe, but true. It happened over a year ago, when I was at Forestview's first soccer game of the season. I was standing beside Ruby when the game finished. Up until then, Ruby and I had only been the kind of friends who nodded to each other in the halls and smiled. So I was surprised when she asked if I wanted to stay after school and watch the game with her.

We stood together near the end of the field, a safe distance from a crowd of older girls who were holding the guys' jackets and stuff. I hadn't been around guys much, especially older guys, so I was self-conscious, but Ruby shouted and cheered and called the players by their names.

"Half of the team are my cousins," she told me.

When the game finished, the guys were congratulating each other as they ran past us. Linc nodded at Ruby and then looked straight at me. He slowed down.

"Vik, right?" he said. He was close enough that I felt heat

coming off his body, and that's when a huge surge of sweaty man smell hit me.

I'd seen him before. I mean, who could miss him? But up close? Oh my! The way he smiled! And then the sound of my name coming out of his mouth. By the time I could find my tongue and say, "Yeah, Vik," he'd run off to join the rest of his team.

Ruby was laughing. She said I looked like the whitest person she had ever seen in her whole life. I can just imagine because I was feeling so woozy I thought I was going to faint. From his scent, I mean. It almost knocked me over. His was not a locker-room stinky smell. It was like inhaling very expensive perfume.

Besides, it's not every day that a guy like Linc Amos slows down long enough to pay attention to a girl like me. He was in grade eleven, tall, gorgeous, First Nations, athletic. No contest; he was the hottest guy in the school. I was a tiny bit cute, I guess, and like Ruby had pointed out, very white. Not hot whatsoever. And, as of grade ten, yet to be discovered by guys of any sort. The situation was simple: Linc was way out of my reach, and there had to be some mistake.

Then my phone rang.

"Vik, right?"

I looked down the field. He was standing with one hand on his hip, the other on his phone. He was looking up the field at me with a wide grin on his face.

"Yeah, Vik," I said, stunned.

"You girls want a ride?"

Ruby got in the back seat of his minivan. I sat up front and put my backpack on my lap. I hugged it with both hands. I had a sense that I should try to look as normal as possible. But there was nothing normal about riding in a car with a boy. No boy had ever asked me if I wanted a ride. And if one had, Dell and Bert would have gone ballistic if they found out.

Truthfully, I was so totally intoxicated by the smell in Linc's van that I still can't remember what happened on the way home.

Ruby told me later that I said something about my name being Victoria Buckingham, like the palace in England. She told me that, all things considered, I didn't make a complete fool of myself. Which was lucky for me.

I read that humans excrete pheromones, which are supposed to be invisible and undetectable. They are airborne molecules that make a chemical reaction and can affect the behaviour of other people. I guess that's what happened to me, except there was nothing invisible about Linc's pheromones. It was like they had legs and got up and almost knocked me over. Like they invaded my clothes and crawled inside my heart and my body.

When we stopped in front of my house, I fumbled around with the door handle. He reached across. His hot, warm, heavenly smelling body spread itself across me, squishing my backpack into my lap. He opened the door and sat back up. I stuttered some kind of "Bye" as I slid out of the car.

By then I was sure he thought he had paid attention to the wrong girl. I was equally sure I was a mindless loser. But I also knew that my life had completely changed and nothing would be normal again.

He reached across again and shut the door behind me. He said, "Later." Ruby crawled into the front seat and shouted, "Bye, Vik." And they drove away.

My legs felt soggy, as if they would buckle underneath me. I stumbled to the front stairs and grabbed the rail to keep me standing up. My head was still high from his scent. Then my cell rang. I scrabbled around in my pocket and pressed *Talk*.

"Vik, right?"

It was Linc.

"Yeah, right," I stuttered. "Right. Vik, that's me."

My brain thought, *If I keep stammering like this, he's going to think I'm an idiot and never speak to me again*, but what I said was "Three times and you'll be out." I don't know why such a stupid thing came out of my mouth, but he laughed, and the sound of his laughter calmed me down. Pretty soon I started to get the feeling back in my legs.

"Come on," he said. "Don't tell me I've struck out before I even get started."

"No," I said, feeling stupid. "Of course not. That was a dumb thing to say."

"How about I come over later?" he said.

He didn't understand. No guy had ever come to my house to see me. The truth was, no one at all had ever come to my house to see me. It was just not the sort of place to invite friends. It wasn't the house so much as Bert and Dell, otherwise known as my father and mother.

So I said to him, "How about I meet you at TJ's?"

Linc set a time, but I was only half listening because I was imagining what Bert would do if he knew that I was planning to meet a First Nations boy at the store.

I was in such a panic about the trouble I would be in that I couldn't remember the time we agreed to. So when we hung up, I ran to the store right away and waited for a couple of hours for him to show up.

After that, I found a way to see Linc almost every day. He was my love. It didn't matter what Bert thought about it. Linc was my life. From then on I was always waiting—phone in hand. A nanosecond after it rang I'd take a deep breath, and then suddenly I would feel his body almost touching me.

Nice story. Love stories are always good until things begin to go wrong.

One Month Later

Vik

"Nice sign," Linc said as he moved it off the side of the road and onto the lawn.

I stood back and took another look.

Save Our Streams

Meeting first Friday of the month

7:00-8:30 pm

Everyone welcome

"Do you think it looks too formal? Will people think I'm overdoing it?"

Linc rolled his eyes. Both of us knew everyone always thought I was overdoing it.

But at our last SOS meeting before summer break, the committee had agreed to pay to get the sign painted. Now, looking at it by the side of the road in the reserve subdivision, I had second thoughts. The last thing I needed was to look more obsessive than I already did.

Linc said, "Don't worry about it, babe."

He held his arms out and I did a swan dive into them. Then Linc scooped me up off my feet—my absolutely favourite thing—and carried me over to the front stairs of his house.

"It took me twenty minutes to get here," I said. I checked my stopwatch again and saw it was actually twenty minutes and twenty-two seconds, but I decided not to correct myself. "No jogging, just a fast walk. I didn't want to get all sweaty. Pretty good, don't you think?"

"Excellent, you're a walking machine."

"No, seriously, it took me almost twenty-five minutes last time."

"Babe, you're amazing."

I knew Linc didn't think I needed to exercise so much. But it helped me stay balanced, and the more out of balance I felt, the more I exercised. It worked.

"There's just so much for SOS to do. We can't slack off now. Once we get this project finished, we need to keep the momentum going for the work farther upstream or everything will just peter out." I stopped talking only long enough to take a breath. "I talked to Adrian from the nursery, and it's all set. The seedlings were delivered up the mountain today. And Ian from Community Stream Corp is going to meet us tomorrow morning at eight, up at the stream, to show us how to plant the seedlings."

SOS might have been my big idea, but without Linc we'd be nowhere. It wasn't until he and his mom, Sandy, came on board that the group got its wheels.

"Okay, okay. But for now, just hold on." Linc pulled me closer and nestled his face into my neck. "How about a kiss?"

"Sorry, sorry, sorry."

I gave him a quick kiss that whisked over his lips and skimmed his cheek. "You know what happens to me when I get excited about the stream. I can't stop planning. And tomorrow is the biggest day of all."

He pressed his hands on my cheeks and looked into my eyes.

"Don't worry. It'll all work out. Now how about a little attention for me."

I kissed my finger and placed it on his lips. Sometimes I wondered what Linc saw in me. He told me that he'd watched me around the school since we were kids, and that it was the way I always stayed to myself that made him want to get to know me. "I was curious," he said. "You were cute and quiet, and I was sure there was something I was going to like. And I was right. I don't just like you. I love you." It was hard for me to believe most of the time—a guy like Linc in love with a girl like me? He didn't know it then, but in my case, quiet meant messed up. If it weren't for Linc, I'd still be a total loner.

By seven-fifteen, all seven members of the committee had arrived. Sign or no sign, the seven o'clock start turned into seven-fifteen.

Ashley lay on the floor with her legs sprawled across Billy.

"God, you guys," Linc said to them. "Aren't you brother and sister?"

"Shut up, cousin," Ashley said. "You're so gross. I'm not even related to him."

"It's not our fault," Billy said. "Just 'cause Mom got together with Ashley's old man doesn't mean we're siblings." Ashley kissed him on the lips to prove his point. "We got together before our parents did."

Linc threw them a couple of pillows to sit on and brought in a chair from the kitchen for his mom. Sandy sat on the floor instead, cross-legged. She was the only adult I knew who fit in with kids. But like she always said, "Don't you all forget there's a mother in the house." She folded her hands and breathed as if she was at a meditation session.

Someday, I thought, *I'm going to be like her.*

I passed around the agenda I'd printed out and then sat on the big leather recliner that everyone called the Chair's chair.

"Can we call this meeting to order?"

I'd found *Robert's Rules of Order* on the Internet, and it was a lifesaver. It might be almost two hundred years old and a little stuffy, but I needed rules to help me avoid meeting chaos, which was exactly how the room looked.

There were a few snickers.

"I see we're going to have another real white-man kind of meeting," Billy said, looking around at the others for approval.

Point taken. I was the only white person in the room.

"Shut up, Billy," Linc said. "We have the chance to do some really big stuff on this committee. We need to be organized."

"Well, Vik's got you organized, anyways," Billy sneered.

"Leave it alone," Linc warned him.

Much as I tried to ignore him, Billy sometimes got me off my game. I didn't know whether to give up on the formalities or forge ahead the way I had the meeting planned.

"Hey, didn't Jona say he'd be here?" Leon asked.

"For sure," Ashley said. "He told me after school he wouldn't miss it."

"We're going to have an induction ceremony, right?" Leon continued. "Jona will be the newest SOS member."

"Can't anyone read?" Billy said, jabbing his finger at his copy of the agenda. "It's right there before 'other business.' Good thing we have an *agenda*, or nobody would know what was going on."

"Great," Linc said, ignoring Billy. "I was worried Jona might have forgotten." He glanced at me as if I was supposed to be excited about Jona joining us. I was. But there was something about Linc's expression that bothered me.

In less than a month, Linc and Jona had become like new best friends, and although at first I thought Jona had been the one to glue onto Linc, I was beginning to wonder whether Linc was getting a little too stuck on Jona. I'd never seen him so attached to a guy friend before.

I set my copy of *Robert's Rules* on my lap. Just knowing it was there might help me organize my brain.

"We could wait another fifteen minutes or so," Linc suggested. "He's probably on his way."

"Show of hands," Ruby chimed in. "All in favour of waiting for Jona, hands up."

I loved Ruby. She was the only real girlfriend I'd ever had, and everyone knew she didn't know when to be quiet, but who was sitting in the Chair's chair, anyway?

"We're already fifteen minutes late," I said. "If Jona was serious about this, he'd be here by now."

"Come on, chill out, Vik," Ashley said. "You're on the reserve now, girl. What's fifteen minutes? We've got all night."

Ruby frowned at me. "Yeah," she said. "A few more minutes won't hurt."

I could feel my eyes burning and my lips starting to quiver. I couldn't risk crying when I opened my mouth. I took a deep breath, hoping it would calm me down.

Luckily, Linc got the picture. "Why don't we get started, and Jona can join in when he gets here? That works for me."

There were a few grumbles, but no one disagreed.

"Good," I said. "I call this meeting to order."

"Order, order, order," Billy said under his breath.

I tried to ignore him and asked, "Does anyone have anything to add to the agenda?"

Billy mumbled something I couldn't hear, and everyone else shook their heads.

"Okay, then. I have just a short update as Chair. Good news first. Ian says that because of our work, he expects to see salmon coming back up as early as next season. This means we have met one of the main objectives of SOS. Mixed news next. We got a Community Works grant again this year but didn't get the Regional District grant we were hoping for."

I nodded in Sandy's direction, giving her the floor.

"Thanks, Vik. The grants were also part of my treasurer's report, but I'm happy to report that I was talking to the folks at the school, and they put me in touch with another grant opportunity that sounds like a good possibility. But first, I want to say thank you for all your hard work on this, Vik." That started a whole round of congratulations, with everyone thanking everyone.

Billy sat up and flexed his arms. "Let's be serious. Ashley couldn't have lived since the last meeting without me."

She punched his arm and laughed. "Could so."

The two of them always carried on like that, but tonight I wasn't in the mood for it.

"Order! We need to keep this meeting moving along."

"Order," Billy said, mimicking me.

Sandy gave the financial report, which was good. The bottle drive and silent auction we had held in the spring raised more than we expected, and we were starting to get some private donations from people in Carterton. She gave us a few details about the other grant, which we would be able to apply for the minute we had completed our first major project. Photos of the newly planted area and a signed letter from Ian were all we needed.

"I'm on it," Ashley said. "I'll take all the shots we need tomorrow."

Ruby reported next on the rides and food and coffee she'd arranged for our trip up the mountain. Leon, now our group secretary, noted everything in the minutes.

I looked around the room. The meeting was back on track,and everyone seemed happy. "Tomorrow might be one of the best days of our lives," I said. "I used to feel sick every time I looked up the hill and saw the clear-cut around the stream. It was like an open sore that no one cared about." Everyone was nodding, so I carried on. "I used to lie awake at night and worry about the fish, and the damage Carter Forestry did to our mountain. What SOS is doing for Chutlow Stream might be a drop in the bucket, but at least now I know we can do *something.*"

Even Billy nodded. "She's got that right," he said. Coming from him, that was a big compliment.

We were almost wrapping up when there was a knock on the door. Jona burst in before anyone had time to answer it.

"Late and sorry," he said. "Really late and really sorry. It's not a good way to get started, but I got mixed up and thought it was seven-thirty until I read the sign outside." He looked at his cell. "Truth is, I fell asleep, so now I'm even late for seven-thirty."

I said, "Better late than never." Although I wasn't sure I believed it. It was seven forty-nine and the meeting was almost finished.

Jona plopped himself down on the sofa between Ruby and Linc. Linc slid over to make room. Ruby looked a little annoyed that they were all smunched together in a tight space, but not Linc. He seemed to be liking it fine.

Jona fished around in his backpack. "I don't want to interrupt. I mean, is it okay? I brought a bunch of books you guys might want to look at."

I looked at the agenda and then up at the group. We were almost finished the committee business, and everyone looked interested in what he was saying, so I waited for him to pass the books around.

"Maybe you could start a lending library or something like that," Ruby said. "It would be great if we all got to know what's going on out there."

"Sure. We could do that," Jona said.

Sandy offered some shelf space for the library, and Ruby began to instruct Leon on how to record who borrowed books. Jona was leaning over the book he'd given Linc and was turning pages like he was reading Linc a bedtime story.

"You guys have to see this book," Linc said, looking totally mesmerized. "It's full of one totally gruesome photo of a clear-cut after the other."

He held it up so we could see a few of the photos. It looked like a medical journal with gross pictures of skin conditions.

"It's one thing to be up the mountain and right inside the clear-cuts," he said. "From a distance you get a whole different perspective."

Jona kept turning the pages and showing things to Linc. I couldn't take my eyes off the way the two of them looked together. They were like little kids or best girlfriends. Right from the start it had been different between the two of them. Even the way Jona looked at Linc when they first met. I'd thought at first he was shy, but it wasn't that at all. Jona liked Linc.

Then I got to thinking about the way Linc had rubbed Jona's

neck and spoken into his ear at the beach that first day of school. That hadn't been Linc's usual massage. Not with the way Jona leaned into each stroke. And Linc looked way too comfortable. More than comfortable. Since then they'd never stopped texting each other or phoning. It was as if Linc couldn't wait for Jona to call. Add to that the fact that they had been hanging out almost every day. And when was the last time Linc and I were together without Jona?

"Any other business?" I asked. By now, all I could think about was getting out of there.

Ashley shifted off the pillow onto her knees. "Vik, what about our plan?"

"Oh yeah," I said. "I forgot."

"Forgot" wasn't quite the right word. I just didn't feel excited anymore, not about Jona.

"Go ahead, Ash," I said. "You can do it."

Ashley ran out into the kitchen, where we had stashed a cupcake. She came back in and presented it to Jona. "I don't know what to say except we are all super happy you are joining SOS."

Jona looked flustered. "Thanks. Doesn't everyone get one?"

"Just you," Ashley said.

"Does anyone else want a bite, then?" Jona asked. "Ruby?"

She looked like she wanted one, but she shook her head.

Jona held it up to Linc's mouth so he could take a bite. Was it really happening? Linc opened his mouth and took a bite as everyone hooted. With the way the two of them were acting, I almost expected him to lick the icing off Jona's fingers.

"I'm duly noting that in the minutes," Leon said. He held up his laptop. "It's all in here. Jona shared his cupcake with Linc." Everyone burst into laughter.

I tried to think about anything other than how my boyfriend was snuggling with a guy right in front of my eyes. And to make it worse, I was sure Ruby and Ashley had noticed as well.

Ruby elbowed Jona. "Do you want to say something?"

"Um, I just hope I can be some kind of help with what SOS is doing. I'm a book nerd, and before I got to Carterton I'd read all the books I could find on the environment. When Vik told me about this group on the first day of school, I thought it was too good to be true. I knew I'd found someone else who cared as much about the environment as I do, and she was actually doing something about it. And now there are all of you."

"We're super excited about having a new member too," Ruby said. "Let's hear it for Jona."

I didn't want to hear it for Jona. In fact, I was beginning to wonder where I fit in the whole club.

"I don't know if this falls into 'other business' or not," I said. I thought for a few seconds and then decided to continue. "But I read somewhere that after a year a group should take a look at its organization—the chair, the secretary, the finance—and just to let you know, I'm willing to step down as Chair if someone else wants to take over my position. I just want to put it out there so you can think about it."

Linc looked shocked. But Sandy jumped in and said, "Good leadership, Vik. If anyone wants to do the finance, they are welcome to it."

"How about Jona for Chair?" Leon said. "Go for it, bro. You can do it."

"Thanks." Jona looked stunned. "Someday, maybe. For now I'm good just joining your group." He stopped and looked around the room and then at the stack of books he had pulled out of his bag. "I mean, I've never seen a real salmon-spawning stream or even been up a mountain. Books are great, but—"

Linc interrupted him and said, "You would make a great Chair."

What was he thinking? I could have killed him. I tried to catch his eye so he'd know how peeved I was, but Jona had put one of the books on Linc's lap, and Linc started flipping the pages.

"Any more discussion?" I asked. I had been so glad Jona was joining SOS at first. Now I didn't know what to think about him. "If not, all in favour of bringing this meeting to a close?"

Everyone put up their hand.

"Passed," I said.

There was a round of clapping, and then Linc announced, "Party here tomorrow night when the planting job is done."

I was beginning to dread spending the whole day with Linc and Jona, and a party was the last thing I wanted.

Linc

Even though the meeting was over, I couldn't take my eyes off the book Jona had handed me. Page after page of photos of what looked like war zones. Jona kept telling me bits of information on where and when the cuts had taken place.

"Did you know that only thirty percent of the earth is covered in trees?" he said.

I had never thought about that before.

"And that the planet will be completely deforested in a hundred years if we keep up our current logging practices?"

Jesus. I tried to imagine the planet with no trees. My own kids could live that long. But could *anyone* live without trees?

"More than half the rainforests are already gone," Jona continued.

"How do you know so much about trees?" I asked him. "Do you spend all day reading books?"

He shrugged. "I read a lot when I'm not making music."

"Really?" I said. "What do you play?"

"Guitar."

"Do you write your own songs?"

"Yeah. Mostly I sing my own tunes."

"That's impressive. Why didn't you say so earlier?"

"I didn't think anyone was interested."

"I'm interested. Although the only things I know how to play are soccer and basketball." I shook my head, thinking how backward I must sound to him. "I have to admit, you won't find me doing much singing, or even reading, for that matter."

"No worries," he said. "Just say the word and I'll teach you how to play if you want. Maybe you could teach me a few game skills. My athletic ability is pretty damn sad."

I closed the book and held it out to him.

"Keep it," he said. "It's for you."

"Wow. Thanks. And thanks for the offer to teach me guitar. I've never thought about playing an instrument before."

I looked around the room and realized Vik wasn't there.

"Where's Vik?" I asked.

No one paid much attention to my question. I checked in the kitchen, knocked on the bathroom door. Leon. "Sorry."

Finally I found her on the porch, sitting on the top stair.

"Good meeting, babe."

"Yeah."

"I love what you said about your dreams for SOS. I'm stoked about finishing this project. Then we can decide on how to do the next one."

"Yeah, right," she said. She had her chin in her palms and didn't even move her head to look at me.

I put my arms around her shoulders and whispered in her ear. "How about that private time you promised me?"

She balled her fingers up and then started wringing her hands together. "I phoned Dell. She'll be here in a few minutes to drive me home."

"Dell? What?" Apparently I had missed something important. Usually Vik did everything in her power to avoid asking her mom for anything.

"I need to go home, and it's too dark to walk."

I bent down to give her a kiss and met her lips as they slipped past. She sat straight-backed. "I'm going to walk over to the beach so she can pick me up on the road." Vik didn't need to remind me that her mother wouldn't drive onto the reserve.

"Why don't I drive you home, like usual."

"Don't worry about it."

Vik didn't sound mad. Just distant. But the longer we sat there, as if we were frozen, I thought about how, a couple of days earlier, she'd walked out of the lunchroom without an explanation. And she'd started to take off early after school if Jona and I were lifting weights in the fitness room. My mind did a crazy gymnastics thing of trying to figure out what might be the common thread.

But thinking about that kind of stuff just messed up my head. "C'mon, let me drive you home," I said.

She slipped out from under my arms and walked down the stairs.

"I'll talk to you later," she said, her voice chilly.

"Hey, Vik." I followed her for a few steps. "You all right, babe?"

"Yeah, I'm fine. I told you. I just need to go home."

I walked with her along Beach Road until I saw Dell's car slow down.

"Are you sure?"

"Go have fun with your friends."

She opened the car door and got in.

"Hey, Mrs. Buckingham." I threw Vik's mom a wave.

"Hello."

"Bye, Vik."

The car took off, and I was left standing there, wondering what the hell just happened. I put the night into rewind. I wondered what was behind her surprise announcement about reviewing the executive positions, but Mom was right. Vik was a good leader. It was a good move. Otherwise there was nothing I could remember that had gone wrong. Billy was his normal asinine self, but Vik was used to him. I'd done my part to defend her, just like we had promised each other when we first got together. "I'll have your back," I'd say. "And I'll have yours," she'd say in reply. And everybody else in the group had supported her as well. Everyone was all stoked about tomorrow.

God, Vik could be confusing. I walked back to the house, thinking at least I could be sure that tomorrow she'd be over her mood.

Jona

Linc came back into the house, looking like shit, and collapsed in the leather chair. He leaned his head back and closed his eyes. He didn't look like he was going to sleep so much as putting up a *Do Not Disturb* sign.

I knew Vik was upset about something. I figured it could have been because I came in late, when the meeting meant so much to her. Or maybe it was something Linc had done. But who was I to say? I'd had about as much experience with relationships as I had with skydiving and other threatening activities. None. The truth was that I tried to stay away from things that might mess me up, and relationships were definitely in that category.

Ashley and Billy were lying side by side on pillows, playing a video game called *Master Alien Insects*. They were nudging one another and giggling as if they were settling in for a long night. Leon was stretched out on the sofa, flipping through the pages of the *Stein* book.

"This stuff is brutal." He grimaced.

I'd never spent much time hanging out at other kids' houses; this was all new to me. Linc's house was like commune city. Every time I'd been there, people came and went as they wanted and, except for tonight, no one seemed to have been invited.

"Hey, Jona," Ruby called from the kitchen. "Wanna help me make some nachos?"

"Sure," I called back. I joined her, picking up some grated cheese off the counter and reaching for my mouth.

She smacked my hand. "Hands off."

Following Ruby's instructions, I sprinkled peppers and ground beef over the tortilla chips, then the cheese.

"Here." She opened the fridge and passed me some tuna salad and a jar of dill pickles. "Dump this on top."

"Whoa. Doesn't look appetizing to me."

"Don't you know, nachos were invented by some guy who emptied his fridge onto some corn chips and put cheese on top."

"I bet he didn't have tuna salad or dill pickles."

She giggled when she put them back in the fridge. "I guess if he had," she said, "nachos wouldn't be so famous."

I was starving, and the nachos in the oven were starting to smell delicious, but I had words flying around in my head. I needed to get somewhere quiet to write them down before they disappeared.

"I gotta get going."

"No way," Ruby hollered. "You can't go until the nachos are done. And besides, everyone's hanging around tonight. You can't spoil the party."

"Vik's already gone. Plus my mom's going to be home from work soon, and I want to get her something to eat." I didn't know where that comment came from, but it rolled off my tongue with no problem at all.

"Okay. Say hi to her for me." She tossed her hands in the air. "But you'll be missing a good thing." She took the nachos out of the oven and put the tray on the kitchen table. "You're right," she said, after tasting one. "They're better without dill pickles. But I still think the tuna salad might have been good."

I pulled a loaded chip off the top of the pile and twisted the cheese strings around until I had a chance of getting it into my mouth.

"Next time," she said.

"With fried eggs and wasabi."

"Gross."

"Ketchup, relish, and mustard."

"No," she said. "With Smarties, chocolate sauce, and whipped cream."

We were laughing like a couple of little kids. *If I had a sister,* I thought, *I'd want one like Ruby.*

I grabbed a few more chips. "Thanks. They are great. I'll see you tomorrow morning early, up on the mountain."

As I passed through the living room, Linc opened his eyes. "Sure you don't want to stay for a while?"

"Love to. But I have to get home to make dinner for Mom," I said. "And I want an early night. Ready for tomorrow. You know."

"I hear you. I'm feeling the same way," he said. "I'll pick you up at seven-fifteen. How's that?"

"Extremely early, but I'll be ready. Anything I need to bring?"

"Gardening gloves, if you have them. The rest of the tools are up at the site."

"Gardening gloves?" I snickered. "Really?"

He laughed. "No sweat. I have a few extra pairs."

"See you."

Outside, the moon lit up the reserve as if the place was lined with streetlights. A couple of dogs strolled down the middle of the road, but everything else in the village felt like it had gone to sleep. Surf pounded on the beach, and I could just make out the way-off rush of the river dropping over the falls before it flowed under the bridge and into the bay.

I walked to the end of Linc's street, across Beach Road, and then through a dark stand of cedar trees. There wasn't a human sound other than the faint hum of a car in the distance. I climbed over some driftwood and sat down on the cool sand. Moonlight lit up the bay all the way out to the Pacific Ocean. It boggled my mind to think that the next place on the planet was Japan. Except maybe for the garbage dump the size of Europe that was circling around out there somewhere.

Before I got too depressed about the disaster humans had made of the oceans, I sucked in a monster breath of air. It was beautiful. Clean. Crystal-clean compared to Vancouver. My lungs were nearly bursting with supercharged air. *Humans made a mess of the earth,* I thought, *but humans can clean it up. And I'm going to be part of the cleanup. I'm not just reading about climate change anymore. I'm going to make a difference.*

I took my notebook and a pen from the seat pocket of my jeans. Words raced around in my head. They might be a poem or a song if I could just let them settle down. I started to write. I loved the way the pen formed words across the paper...

Don't frown You're a clown.
Who knows the road to Carterton?
Who knew there was one?
Can I reuse...did I lose my muse in this bush town?
Never mind, rewind
We're here momma dear
let's make it clear...

My gut started to tense up, and the words stopped. I put my pen down and closed my eyes. I used to freak out when my brain blocked words, until I read somewhere that it is part of the creative process. *Chill and let yourself feel the tension,* I said to myself. I thought about my fingertips until I could feel them tingle. Then I followed the tingle right up my arms. I imagined my elbows and shoulders, my chin, my lips, my nose. Everything was loose. Pretty soon I could hear music coming up from my belly. I started tapping my toe.

"Hey."

Holy. I just about crapped myself. I opened my eyes and looked up to see Linc towering over me. The moonlight outlined his shoulders and curly hair with a silver glow.

"I thought you were going home."

"I was." I wasn't going to admit I had made that up. "I thought you were going to sleep."

"I was. Actually, I wasn't. I just didn't feel like talking anymore, so I shut my eyes. I walk this beach at night whenever I've got things to think about. Sorry for interrupting you."

"Hey, no, it's me who invaded your space. But seeing that we're both here"—I pointed with my chin to the space beside me—"how about you sit down? My neck is getting sore looking up at you like that."

He kicked off his shoes and leaned against the same log as me. He buried his feet in the sand, then lifted them up to let the sand filter between his toes.

"Got anything you wanna share?" he asked, staring at the page.

"No," I said, wondering if I should cover it up. What the hell would he think about my writing? "Words are just process.

They wouldn't mean anything to you. I mean, they don't even mean anything to me most of the time."

I expected him to say "No worries, don't bother then," but he closed his eyes as if he was waiting for me to start. "Try me."

"Well...I guess..." I swallowed a few times and started, "*Don't frown You're a clown. Who knows the road to Carterton? Who knew there was one?*" My voice deepened. "*Can I reuse... did I lose my muse in this bush town? Never mind, rewind.*"

Out of the corner of my eye I watched as Linc's foot picked up the rhythm. He put his fists in the sand and hunched himself up into a straight sitting position, leaving his arm touching mine. "*We're here momma dear let's make it clear...*"

Can he feel every last hair on my arm standing on end?

By the end, I wished I had written more, so I reread the last bit. "*Let's make it clear.*"

"Wow, that's good." He didn't open his eyes, but he smiled. "Tell me more. I don't really know anything about you."

I swallowed again, hard. "Talking about me isn't exactly something I'm comfortable with. You know, we all have our family secrets."

He opened his eyes. "Not around my place. Haven't you noticed?" Linc laughed. "Everyone knows everything. I guess I like it that way. Mom always says that family secrets take too much work to keep hidden."

God, did I know that was true. But in a way it was backward as well. Secrets are also too much trouble to tell.

"I don't even know where I'd begin."

He shifted down slightly so his head and neck rested against the log. "I'm not going anywhere," he said. "Just start talking."

After a long pause, I began. "Well, Mom and I lived on

the east side of Vancouver. You know. You've heard of the place. Not exactly high class, but it was where we lived until Aunt Lonnie changed all that. Aunt Lonnie is my mom's sister, from Toronto. She used to call my mom and me in Vancouver and warn us when she was coming to visit. It was a good thing, because it gave my mom a chance to get her shit together and get up off the sofa. And let me tell you, that was a major event, because Mom lay on that sofa day and night."

I glanced down at Linc to see how he was reacting to what I was saying. But he was relaxed, as if he had heard worse. His long eyelashes rested on his cheeks, and his lips were full—pouty. He was stunning, and it made me nervous. I'd always heard that an audience of one was the same as an audience of a hundred, but not this *one*.

"Aunt Lonnie never stayed long—two or three days, max—but man, it seemed like forever because she was like a hawk, watching everything we did."

I did a high, nasal voice and mimicked her. "*You call this bathroom clean? Why don't you get a new fry pan? Good God, how do you two even fry an egg?*"

Linc laughed. "She sounds like a winner, your aunt," he said.

That stung. "Actually, she's cool," I said quickly. "She doesn't have kids, so I'm kind of like the son she never had. She buys me stuff that would blow your mind—computers, games, concert tickets, tickets to hockey games, all my guitars. Lately we've been shopping together online. We're both into coloured shoes and cardigans."

"Well, that explains a thing or two," Linc said.

"Yeah—I do a pretty good Toronto hipster impression for a welfare kid from the east side of Vancouver. Anyway, Aunt

Lonnie showed up unannounced one day, and the place was looking like the dump it really was, and Mom wasn't looking so good either. I had been playing music in this guy's basement, and I didn't get home until after midnight. By that time, Aunt Lonnie had been stewing around the house for hours and was almost out of her mind. As soon as I walked in the door, she got right up in my face for not telling her about how Mom and I really lived. It all got bent out of shape, and she ended up threatening to take me back to Toronto with her and force Mom to get medical help. I'd been looking after Mom since I was a little kid. I knew I wasn't doing a great job of it, but I wasn't about to let her separate us. It didn't take long for Aunt Lonnie to get the picture. Finally she offered to find Mom a job somewhere so we could start over.

"So, da dum, here I am." I tossed my arms out as if I was taking a bow.

Linc was sitting up with his elbows on his knees and his eyes focused on me. I was surprised he was still interested.

"That's quite a story," he said. "I can't believe anyone would choose Carterton to give someone a new start. It's like you moved from addict street to redneck and Indian country. I hope it works out for you."

"Jesus, just when I was starting to like it here."

"I don't want to burst your bubble. I like the place myself, but Vik hates it. She says Carterton is like the places in those dystopia novels everybody reads...sort of like what happens after the end of the world. Carterton died after the mill shut down, and now it's your basic ghost town."

I put my arms up into an X. "Please, no more heavy shit. Just let me be deceived and learn to love the place."

I didn't tell him that I'd read about the guy who'd owned the mill, George Carter, and that he was off somewhere basking in the sun on all the money he'd made. I was sure Linc knew that already.

He sat up a little straighter. "As far as I can see, you're an Indian, but not a redneck."

We both laughed.

"I guess so. My dad was a Mohawk. Mom was a white girl from East Vancouver."

"Kind of like Vik and me."

"I hope your story turns out better than theirs. Mom was sixteen when I was born. She dropped out of school. Dad left when she was twenty with a four-year-old kid to raise alone. And, as she says, she'd lost the love of her life. She sort of checked out, I guess. The good news is, I think she's checking back in."

"That's hardcore," Linc said. He looked thoughtful. "There's not much interaction between the First Nations and white people around here. Vik and I are the only couple I know right now crossing over the line."

"In Vancouver, it didn't seem to matter much. I mean the race thing. Everyone is from somewhere else. The city has people from every colour of the rainbow dating people from every other colour," I said.

"Not here. There are two sides to this town, First Nations and whites. Other than the Basi family, who keep to themselves. And the two sides don't like each other very much either. But it's no freaking wonder. They don't even know each other. And as far as I can tell, most people aren't trying very hard to change that."

Maybe the First Nations/white thing was trouble for Mom and Dad, I thought. *Maybe that's why I don't know any of my*

Mohawk relations. But how would I know? Rule number one in our family: no talking about Dad.

"You still haven't told me why you chose Carterton," Linc said.

"It was more like a case of having no choice. This place was the deal Aunt Lonnie put together, and it surprised the hell out of me that Mom went for it. Aunt Lonnie knows Bill Henderson, the guy who owns the lodge, and it just so happened that he had a beat-up old trailer and a job for a cleaner. I guess they're old friends, and as a favour to Lonnie he agreed to give Mom a chance. So here we are."

"Crazy. Glad it all turned out that way." He gave me a pat on my leg and jumped up. His touch sent a sizzling shock wave up my thighs. I stayed sitting down for a few seconds to let them cool off. Good thing he was looking the other way and didn't see my reaction.

I checked the time on my cell. Twelve-ten. "I better get home," I said. "Seven-fifteen is coming up soon."

He shook the sand off his pants. "Right."

We parted. Him going one way. Me the other. The moon made it feel like we'd met in the middle of the day.

Linc

As I walked home from the beach, I kept thinking about how my mom was right way too often. "Assume anything, and you make an ass out of you and me" was a favourite expression of hers. Right again, Mom.

A Vancouver hipster is exactly what I had thought Jona was. But who would have imagined the rest of his story?

I hadn't wanted Jona to think I was staring at him as he spoke, but I couldn't look away. He was an awesome poet. And in spite of all the personal shit he'd been through, his face looked calm. I didn't want to miss a word. I wanted him to keep talking. There weren't many guys who were willing to talk so straight up like that. Secrets, like Mom said, were better told, but, holy, that was intense stuff.

Yeah, no kidding I hope Vik and I turn out better than Jona's parents, I thought. But one thing I was sure of. I was never walking out on my family like his dad did. There was no damn way.

Vik and I were another story. What was eating her up lately? She had gone from being super excited about going up the mountain to being uptight and angry about something. God, sometimes I couldn't figure that girl out.

I got thinking about secrets and how much Vik hated talking about her family. The truth was, I didn't like hearing about it. She wasn't calm about it, like Jona. And her stuff was so bloody heavy, it freaked me out. Like the day Bert caught Vik and me lying together on her bed. We weren't even doing anything, but he flung the door open and started hollering at the top of his lungs. I flew off the bed and dodged under his arm. He came after me and chased me down the hall and out the door.

"Fucking Indian," he shouted. "I find you messing with my daughter again, I'll kill you."

He slammed the door, and I started the van to take off, though I hung around on the driveway for a few minutes. I didn't want to leave Vik in there, but she didn't come out and there was nothing more I could do.

Later, she showed me the red marks on her face under her makeup. She said he'd dragged her out into the living room, threw her on the sofa, and slapped her around. I didn't know what to say to her. I mean, what *can* you say in a situation like that? From then on I just stayed out of Bert's way.

I got thinking about the other time with Bert that was really bad. Vik said she'd locked her bedroom door because he was going ballistic on her. He'd slammed on it for like an hour or two. When she was telling me, she was crying hard and couldn't stop. But when I tried to calm her down, it just got worse. It was like a super-bad reality show, and in spite of how bad I felt for her, there wasn't a damn thing I could do.

By the time I got home from the beach, I just wanted everything to be right again between us like it used to be. I wanted to hold Vik and tell her I loved her. I wanted to be there for her, but it felt like my love just couldn't be enough.

Linc to Vik: `Hey, babe. U there?`

I smiled into the phone and clicked a selfie.

Linc to Vik: `Here's me saying I love U`

Vik

I was awake when my phone rang at seven. I let it repeat its jingle over and over. Five. Six. Seven rings. Silence.

Usually I'd be lunging for the phone, dying to hear Linc's "Hey, babe."

But there I was, wrapped in my comforter like it was a cocoon, with my pillow over my head to keep the light out. I didn't want to be awake. I sure didn't want to be talking to Linc.

Four minutes of peace and then it started again. I scrunched my knees together and squeezed my eyes shut, hoping that would make the noise less annoying.

"Shut up," I said out loud. "Just shut the freaking hell up!"

I couldn't shut the stupid phone off, though, because I needed to know Linc wanted to talk to me.

Vik, give yourself a break, I told myself. *Linc loves you. You love Linc. Sniff the T-shirt!*

I pulled his shirt out from under my pillow. He'd given it to me as a joke after I told him that the first time I smelled him, I fell in love with him. After almost a year, I was sure the shirt still smelled like him.

But the other voice in my head was louder. *You know crap from crap. What kind of whack-job keeps her boyfriend's sweaty T-shirt in a ball under her pillow? You're a wimp. You can't face the fact Linc would rather be with Jona than with you.*

When I was a kid, I thought I was crazy when I had long conversations with myself. But in Mrs. Wong's life-skills class in grade nine, I learned that self-talk could be useful. It was never totally successful, though. On a good day it could be like a train crash and knock my mind hard enough to send it off the tracks where it had gotten stuck, so I could see things from a different perspective. Otherwise, it was like an annoying big sister, always wanting to argue with me. For now, it worked better than nothing.

I buried my face in the shirt and breathed in. That scent filled my head with good thoughts—Linc loved me. Maybe I could get up after all.

The phone went quiet, then rang again.

How are you going to save the stream if you don't get out of bed? My self-conversation started up. *C'mon, Vik. This is important.*

Then the backtalk butted in. *You are so pathetic. What makes you think you and your useless friends can make a difference?*

I balled the T-shirt up and threw it on the floor. Even if I got out of bed and pulled myself together, I couldn't exactly tell Jona I didn't want him to come with us. The rides had been arranged by Ruby the night before.

My cell beeped. A text message.

Linc to Vik: `Answer??`

I deleted it and seven more without looking at them. I shoved the phone under my pillow.

I wanted to text back *Why do you need me? Take Jona up the hill if he's so cool.*

The phone beeped again. I took it out and stared at the case.

The flag of Great Britain I'd thought was so great when I bought it was peeling back around the corners. It looked like crap.

Don't turn the phone over and read his message, I said to myself. *Ignore him.*

But ignoring Linc was impossible. He was the only person I ever really wanted to think about.

Okay, Vik. Deal: you can read the text as long as you promise not to answer.

Linc to Vik: `It's late. I thought u would call and wake me up. Why aren't you answering?`

Vik to Linc: `Just go with Jona`

I clicked *Send* and burst into tears. Jona was who Linc wanted to be with. He didn't have to pretend that he wanted me.

But the next time the phone rang, my need to hear Linc's voice won out. I pressed *Talk.*

"Yeah?" My lips were itchy. A prickly feeling crept up my cheeks and around my ears. I rubbed the back of my hand across my face.

"Hey, Vik. Sorry I'm late. I slept in. Did you get my message? I've been trying to call you. Where were you?"

If you can hear confusion over the phone, that's what I was listening to. It softened me up for a moment. *Maybe nothing is going on between Linc and Jona,* I thought. *Maybe Linc just doesn't get what it looks like when the two of them are together.*

"Vik? Vik?"

Not a chance. Linc was naïve about a lot of things, relationships among them, but I'd seen him sitting close to Jona. He liked it. There was no doubt about what was going on.

"What?"

"I'll swing around and pick you up in half an hour or so."

Who says stuff like that? "I'll swing around."

I reached down, picked up his T-shirt, and buried my face in it. My eyes and nose started to pour, and I thought of reasons why I loved him. I could count on him. He was loyal. Linc helped keep me alive. I couldn't imagine the world any other way.

I rolled off the bed.

"Okay," I snuffled. "I'll be ready."

"Great. I'll get you first, and then we can head past Jona's on our way up the hill."

It was like a switch had been flicked. What was I thinking? Of course. Jona. But why would I want to be part of his new fling? My fingers went loose, dropping my phone onto the floor.

I could hear Linc's muffled voice. He sounded worried. "Vik? Vik? Are you there?"

I crawled back into bed.

A few minutes later he called back. I pressed *Talk*.

He said, "What happened?"

"I don't know. Something went weird with my phone." I might as well have been talking to a loaf of bread. Linc didn't understand one thing about how I was feeling.

"Wow. That was weird. I was worried that you fell or something."

I kept my mouth shut.

"You okay, babe?"

"Yeah. I'll see you soon." I pressed *End*.

It had only been a month since we met Jona, but our perfect relationship had turned into a disaster because of him. It always used to be Linc and me, and now it was Linc and me and Jona. Or maybe it wasn't even me anymore. How did that happen? I'd been looking forward to this day on the mountain for months. We were so close now to having the stream ready for the salmon. How could I not be there?

Vik, are you actually thinking about staying home? Really?

What else could I do? I felt sick at the thought of watching Linc and Jona rubbing shoulders all day.

I pressed my direct line to Linc. Before he had a chance to say hello, I blurted out, "I'm not going."

"What?"

Have your damn friend. I don't care anymore. Why do you even bother to call me? But the words only smashed around in my head. I couldn't say them out loud.

"I'm not going," I repeated.

"But, Vik, I don't get it. This was your idea. The whole plan. Remember what you said last night? Today's the big day."

Of course I remembered. But that was before I knew for sure what was really going on. The eyes Jona made the first day of school...the extra-special back rub and dancing the night of the beach party...the touching, the looking every other time they'd been together. Then, to cap it off, cozying up at the meeting last night right in front of everyone. Who knows what they got up to after I went home.

I cringed to imagine what Ruby and Ashley must have been thinking. They were probably talking about it right now.

"Vik? Are you there?"

"Yeah, it used to be all my idea," I said. "But it's not about me anymore."

I'd never been a super-jealous person. Okay, so I couldn't help being jealous sometimes of girls at school. Who wouldn't be? Linc was the kind of guy who drew girls to him like a magnet. They fell all over themselves, even when he was just being friendly. Add to that he was a total jock, so guys wanted to hang around with him as well. To be honest, with a boyfriend like Linc it was hard *not* being jealous. But he had never given me a reason to mistrust him until now.

"What do you mean?" he said.

I couldn't say "*You like Jona, admit it, Linc.*" In fact, I had trouble forming the thought. I hated saying it even to myself. How could it be true? Linc was my man. I wanted to believe that Jona was the problem, not him. But what do they say? It takes two to tango?

"Why don't you just go with Jona?"

"But we're planting today," he said. "This is what we've been waiting for. Everyone's probably already heading up the hill."

"I know all that. I made the plans, remember?"

"Yeah, so you have to be there. And now we're late, so Jona's hanging around waiting for us. We gotta get going."

"Just go pick him up."

"Vik? What's wrong with you?"

I wanted to say "*What about what's wrong with* you? *Like, for instance, why are you so hooked on Jona? Do you have the hots for him? Is he your new girlfriend?*" But I couldn't get the words out, so I switched my voice from angry to unwell. A pathetic, whiny voice was a skill I had perfected long ago for use with Dell, and it had gotten me dozens of days off school.

"I don't feel very well," I said. "You better go without me. Why don't you just phone me when you get back?"

"Are you sure?" Linc said. His voice turned instantly from confused to sympathetic. "Maybe you just need to have some breakfast or something."

"I don't feel good enough to eat right now," I said.

"Well, okay." Linc sounded disappointed. "I can't believe you're staying home."

I couldn't believe it either, but I couldn't change my mind now.

"I hope you feel better," he said, sounding genuinely worried. "Have a sleep or something. I love you."

I almost said "I love you too," because I did. Instead I choked out "Goodbye." I wished Linc would stay on the line and tell me that Jona didn't mean anything to him. But he didn't.

"Okay. See you when we get back."

He had given up too easily. *Obviously he doesn't really care if you are there, Vik,* the voice inside me said. *He is probably happy that he gets to go with Jona, just the two of them.*

I tried to think of the bright side. Maybe by staying home I could figure out how to get Jona out of our lives. I had to come up with something. All the things I'd liked about him at first—his friendliness, his interest in the environment, the cool way he talked about the world—he was using to get close to Linc, and that made us rivals. Jona wanted what I had, and I wasn't going to fall for his cool-guy approach. He was working on replacing me, taking away the most important person in my life, and I wouldn't let it happen. I couldn't lose Linc or I'd have lost everything.

I sat on the side of my bed. In the mirror across from me, I saw a thin, feeble girl, her shoulders curled as if they were protecting her almost boobless chest. Her stringy blonde hair framed grey eyes that drooped at the outside edges, as if she were permanently pleading for sympathy. It was my lame-ass self.

I thought about an online personality test I'd done that said I was passive-aggressive. It wasn't true. Maybe I wasn't good at telling people what I thought, but I wasn't passive. Sometimes I just lacked courage. There was a big difference. Passive was the condition of being pathetic, but courage could be summoned. Courage was something I intended to find more of so I could fight for what was mine.

I straightened my back, lifted my chin, and stared at myself in the mirror for a few more moments, eye to eye. Had I already lost Linc? To a guy? My stomach turned. I swallowed hard to keep from throwing up.

Victoria Buckingham, I said to myself, *find your damn voice. You won't get what you want if you let Jona take it. Speak up.*

But it was too late. They were gone, together, and I was left at home by myself.

Jona

I stepped out of the trailer onto the porch and took a look at the morning to decide what jacket to wear. What I'd always thought of as Vancouver weather felt better in Carterton. Damp, grey, low clouds, drizzle seemed more at home around the mountains and ocean than smothering the buildings in the city. And, as usual on the west coast, I just had to look the other way and, to the east, the early morning sun cast a glint of golden light across the mountaintops. It was going to be a good day.

I checked my phone. Seven-ten—Linc would arrive in five minutes. I went back inside, got my fleece and knapsack, and shut the door as quietly as possible, but the rusty hinge squeaked. Damn. I didn't want to wake Mom.

Once I was outside, my stomach started doing turns like a dancer, and I realized maybe I was hungry. I pulled the door open, and it groaned again.

"Jonsey?" Mom called from her bedroom. Why would she call me such a ridiculous name when I have a perfectly good name already? I stuck my head in her room.

"Jona, Mom. Remember, it was you who gave me that name," I said. "And sorry for waking you up. It's that damn door. Go back to sleep. I'm going to wait on the porch for Linc."

"I'll call you whatever I want," she said sleepily. "Have a good time, and be safe up there."

"Will do." I leaned over and gave her hand a squeeze. I didn't really care what she called me. The truth was I kind of liked her calling me Jonsey. It meant she was feeling good. "You'll probably be at work by the time I get home this afternoon, so have a good day." I liked the way she was starting to joke with me, too. It was almost as if we were sort of a normal family.

I grabbed a couple of slices of bread and ran back outside. I stuffed breakfast in my mouth, then gulped some water from my flask to wash it down. For all my reading, I realized I knew nothing about real mountains or logging roads, and I couldn't stop thinking about the terrifying pictures I'd seen of steep cliffs and washouts.

By seven-thirty my stomach was doing pirouettes. Had Linc forgotten me? Although I'd only known him for a month, I was sure he was the kind of guy who did what he said he would. What could happen to him out here in nowheresville? Nobody to mug him. Maybe it was something I'd said, something I'd done the night before. I sat down on the trailer stairs with my notebook and pen. *The gods of anxiety are out to get me.* I doodled a sketch of my shoes as I waited for words to come. Was I kidding? Words were prisoners—tied up in knots in my stomach. *Let the dancers have their way with me.*

I knew the dangers of the city, and I knew how to watch out for them, but what did I know about the things that could go wrong here? People think being street savvy means you don't worry about anything. But street savvy means you worry about everything. You just do it cool, eyes in the back of your head, checking around corners. I was an expert at worrying. *Nothing's safe, my friend, but we're good, yeah?*

I refilled my flask from the outside tap and slid my pack on my back, then started walking down the lane. Our trailer was on a dead end, so there was no way I could miss Linc when he came. Once I got to the road, there was only one direction to the reserve, so I kept walking.

I typed in his number on my cell but pressed *End* before the phone rang. I didn't want to look too anxious. Finally my inner logic kicked in—late did not necessarily mean trouble. It could just mean he slept in. God, think about it.

I stepped off the road and took a pee behind a tree. I was buttoning up my jeans when Linc drove by, then pulled into an overgrown driveway. He turned around and stopped beside me.

"I actually found some old garden gloves under the sink," I said as I climbed in. "I had to shake the cobwebs out of them."

He nodded and smiled, and I saw he was talking on his phone.

I mouthed *Sorry.*

His smile faded and he shook his head when he stuck his phone under his thigh. Judging from the confused-guy look on his face, I guessed he'd been talking to Vik.

"Sorry I'm late. I slept in," he said as he accelerated onto the road. He kept his eyes focused straight ahead. "Actually, I don't think I got to sleep until it was time to get up."

"No worries. Better late than never," I said, making a mental note to myself to stop saying that stupid cliché. He didn't seem to hear it anyway.

He turned on some music—country rock, country pop, country classics, what have you. It wasn't what I would have chosen, but at least it helped my stomach dancers to settle.

At the corner, Linc surprised me by turning toward the mountain instead of heading to Vik's place.

"What about Vik? Isn't she riding up with us?"

Linc made a guppy mouth with his lips and shook his head. "She doesn't feel well." He shrugged his shoulders. "I wondered what was going on with her when she didn't call this morning to get me up."

"Wow." I didn't get it. Had I missed something? "That's too bad."

He shrugged again. He made a couple of huffing noises. I figured it had to do with a hard-wired reality. Girls are beyond words, so guys have to revert to primeval sounds and, at best, animal phrases, to describe their confusion.

A few minutes later, Linc called her again.

"Just checking one last time on whether you really want to stay home," he said. "Just say the word, babe, and we'll come back and get you."

I turned my head to give him privacy and watched the trees whiz past, but it's impossible not to overhear someone's conversation when you're in the front seat of a van with him.

"Are you mad?"

I got thinking about counting trees. I'd read that thing about the percentage, but had anyone ever calculated the number of trees that inhabit the planet? People get counted right down to knowing, when a baby's born, that it's the seven-billionth human or some damn thing like that. We count wolves and grizzly bears to figure out how many we can kill. What about trees? Maybe if we knew exactly how many trees there were, we'd think a little more seriously about destroying them.

"I don't know what's up with Vik," Linc said when the call

ended. "Every weekend she wants to go up to the stream. Even when nothing's going on. Then today, when it's the biggest deal, she stays home. I don't get it. You heard what she said last night."

"For sure. She was into it."

Linc's silence seemed like my cue to say something else. But all I could get out was "Humph," followed by a few shoulder shrugs.

He nodded anyway, like we were talking the same language. "Vik would live up at the stream if she could."

"Huh. That's cool."

"I think the stream gives Vik something to fix. She likes things to be right." He laughed. "You might have noticed that last night."

"Yeah. I mean no. I didn't really notice."

"Vik's good at everything she does. A bit of a perfectionist, I guess you'd say. Sort of," he said, as if he was trying to figure her out. "It's just that Billy and some of the others give her a hard time once in a while."

"Do you think that's why she's not coming today?"

"No. Billy wasn't any worse than usual last night."

"Weird."

"So what the hell is going on with her?"

"Huh? You asking me?" I said. If he only knew how damn little I knew about girls. "How does that Jimmy John song go?" I started singing, "*Girls make the boys go crazy, their smiles entice you like a mystery, you can never get enough but she'll trap you with her stuff...*"

I stopped. Would he think I was making fun of him?

"Sorry, man. The song just came to mind. I mean, I wasn't..."

"No sweat." He grinned. "There's no figuring it out when it comes to relationships. Vik and I used to be perfect together. But the last couple of weeks I can't seem to do anything right."

My hand shot out in a fit of sympathy and touched his shoulder. Whoa. I snatched it back. What would happen if they broke up? A blast of adrenalin shot through me. I looked down at my chest and could see my heart pumping, and farther down—God. I was hard. Again. What the hell was going on? It wasn't as if I had a general case of hots for guys. Up until our move to Carterton, I hadn't really thought about either guys or girls in that way. In fact, the idea of sex had occurred to me so rarely that I wondered whether I was normal. I'd thought maybe I was just a late bloomer, but I sure seemed to be blooming now.

"That's too bad," I said. "I mean, too bad that you can't do anything right." Awkward, I thought. But, thankfully, Linc didn't seem to notice.

"And what about Ian, the guy from Community Streams?" he said. "He's supposed to meet us up there to make sure we plant the seedlings properly and don't plant them too close to the banks. And where the hell are the seedlings? Vik's the only one who knows. She made all the arrangements." He threw his hands up, then slammed them back onto the steering wheel. "I can't bloody believe this could go so wrong. This is so not like Vik."

I tried to think of something genius to say, but all I could think of was "girls will be girls" or "girls get to change their minds," which even I knew would not be helpful.

"SOS got started after Vik's class went on a field trip up the mountain," Linc told me. "Her teacher said it would only take a few kids, with the help of some specialists, and they could bring the fish back up the stream. Our first date was actually up here. We hiked up to the stream because Vik was so determined to get a club going. We almost killed ourselves scrambling over the piles of broken trees. It was like some disaster had happened, and Vik and I were the last people standing.

"When we got up there, I couldn't believe it. The stream was just a bunch of muddy puddles and ponds filled with old snags. Vik knelt down and started to cry. I mean, she was really sobbing." He had both hands on the wheel, and his eyes were on the road ahead, but I could tell he was back at the stream, living that moment out in his mind. "After a few minutes, she started screaming, 'They've killed the stream.'" He glanced at me. "She was almost hysterical. It freaked me out."

"Wow." It sounded dumb and inappropriate, but I couldn't think of what else to say.

"I put my arms around her," he said. "And right there I fell in love with her."

"Wow," I said again. "That's a hell of a love story."

I'd never seen this side of Linc, so I wasn't sure what would be helpful. So, like a geek, I launched into a speech on tree planting based on what I'd read.

"You need to plant the seedlings close together when you are back from the stream and spread them out when you get closer to the banks. Like, down the road a few years, you have to think how big the trees will get and how much they will shade the stream. The other thing to think about is how many leaves the trees will drop in the water. Apparently, leaves are good fish food, but only in small amounts. Did you know the most important fish food in streams is algae? You don't want to create an environment that will destroy its growth."

I felt like sticking my fingers in my mouth and pulling my tongue out to shut myself up.

"That's what I've read, anyway," I mumbled. I took a quick worried look at Linc to check whether he was totally bored.

"How do you know all that stuff if you've never been up a mountain before?" he asked.

"Books."

"How many books have you read about this stuff?"

How should I answer? If I told the truth—a hundred books, maybe more—it might sound like I was showing off.

"I don't know. Ten. Well, if we're being honest, more than ten. A lot more than ten."

"Do you want to study biology or something? Like at university?"

Nobody had ever asked me that before, but a future career studying bugs or fish or whatever biologists did wasn't something I pictured. I thought of myself more as a performer. When I thought a little longer about what he'd said, though, the idea got interesting.

"It hasn't been so much a career thing as a Buddhist thing." I tried to say it like being a Buddhist was cool, and like it would explain everything, but Linc looked puzzled. "I mean, don't the Buddhists think that if you put good thoughts out into the universe, you'll change the world? You know, just sitting and meditating will bring about world peace."

"I don't know anything about the Buddhists, but meditating isn't going to help the salmon come upstream."

"Exactly. And I knew it all along. It's just that reading made me think I was doing something. A good delusion can prevent you from going insane about the state of the world."

"I hear you."

"I guess I wanted to do more than just recycle my coffee cups and avoid plastic. You know—to change the world."

Linc turned his head to look at me. "I'm glad you're here."

Linc was so damn real. Like, when does anyone tell you they're glad you're there?

His face got serious, like he was worried about Vik again. I could have told him that he was in for crap from Vik for a few things he'd said at the meeting. For instance, when he said I'd make a good Chair of the committee. You didn't have to know a damn thing about girls to know that she was fishing—*I'll step down if you want me to.* Right answer: *No, no, you're doing a great job. We can't live without you.* Wrong answer: *Hey, yeah, Jona would be a great replacement.* I knew he was steering in the wrong direction when she threw him a look that could kill someone.

I doubted she was too pleased with me either, because of it. And now that I was thinking about Vik, I realized she didn't seem as enthusiastic about knowing me as she had been on the first day of school.

I didn't know what exactly was going on but I was smart enough to know that Vik was majorly unhappy about something. I mulled all this over and watched the trees. The road was a winding corridor of evergreens that, every few minutes, opened up with a wide-angle, throat-grabbing shot of the ocean. Seriously. Cliché as it sounds, it took my breath away. Despite the stuff with Vik, I was feeling close to excellent. If I was honest, I was happy I had Linc all to myself. I mean, I didn't *want* him all to myself. At least, that wasn't the first thing on my mind. But I guess, if I was truthful, it wasn't the last thing either.

All that aside, I'd never really had friends, not close ones. Back in Vancouver, Mom was afraid that someone would get wise to our situation, so she wouldn't let me bring anyone to our apartment. If kids couldn't even come over for a sandwich or to play video games, it was just easier to avoid making friends altogether. The only time I hung out with people was at George's Basement, and those people were my music buddies, not friends.

Since we'd moved to Carterton, things had been better. Mom didn't sit inside all day, staring at the blinds. We had food in the kitchen. I wasn't proud to call our little old trailer home. As houses went, it was a pretty lame-ass excuse for one. But Linc and Ruby had been over a few times while Mom was at work, and they didn't seem to care.

Linc turned up the radio, and there we were, two cool bros driving in a minivan. I started singing at the top of my lungs:

Their words are oh so sweet
They make you think that you're complete
When you're believing that's when they're leaving.

Vik

I must have dozed off after talking to Linc. When I opened my eyes again, I was frozen to the bone. I put my housecoat on over my pajamas and pushed my feet into my bedroom slippers. In the kitchen I poured myself a cup of coffee and sat down at the table, staring out the window over the sink into the grey sky. It was quiet except for the swooshing sound of geese flying low over the house and the dull blast of the foghorn out on the point.

When I heard Bert and Dell moving around in their bedroom, I thought about going for a run to get out of the house. But the thought only lasted about one second before all I could see was Linc and Jona driving up the mountain. I imagined them sitting side by side in Linc's van with the music cranked. They'd be laughing and talking. What were they saying?

The front seat was mine. Linc's rule. No one got to call shotgun in the van if I was there. He told everyone, "My babe sits up front with me." Even when Billy fought for the seat, Linc wouldn't start the van until I was in front.

I cringed at the thought of Jona sitting in my place. I should have been there, not drinking a cup of bad coffee at home with Bert and Dell. And unless I figured out how to hold on to Linc, Jona would be sitting up front all the time.

Self-talk went back and forth in my head. *Envy is one of the seven deadly sins for a reason. It'll mess you up. You gotta stop worrying about Jona.* Then I told myself, *Being stupid and naïve isn't going to get you anywhere. You have to face the facts.*

That was the trouble, though. I didn't have any facts. Just a feeling. Only one month ago, Jona seemed like the coolest person I'd ever met. I couldn't get enough of him. I thought I had met a kindred spirit—someone who wanted to change the world. Whenever I saw him, we talked about the stream. Maybe I should have gotten the hint that first morning, the way everyone was staring at him. Guys and girls were both attracted to him. He didn't have any trouble at Carterton like I thought he would. He didn't need me. But how the hell could I know that Linc would be the one to get starry-eyed over the guy?

I sipped my coffee. Dell must have made it hours earlier. It was gritty and tasted like shit, and it wasn't even hot.

I shook out the placemats and laid them symmetrically around the table. Three of them, as if our family ever sat down together to eat. The fourth placemat was in the middle, cafeteria style. I lined up the salt and pepper, paper napkins, sugar bottle, and squirt ketchup, then picked up the saucer Dell used for an ashtray and put it on the counter near the back door.

Linc's number lit up my cell.

I pressed *Talk*. "Yeah."

"Just checking one last time on whether you really want to stay home," he said. "Just say the word, babe, and we'll come back and get you."

Oh, really, we'll *come back and get you.* When did Linc turn into a "we"?

"No. You guys don't need me. All you have to do is find the seedlings and plant them. I don't feel well."

"Are you serious?"

"Yeah. I'm serious." I'd never been more serious in my life. I was missing the day I had been waiting for. My boyfriend was with someone else. And SOS didn't need me anymore. How serious could I get? "Just come over when you get down the mountain," I said.

"Are you mad?" Linc's voice was cautious.

"No. Just sick. I must have caught some kind of bug. I'll be okay. Plant a tree for me?"

"I will, babe," Linc said. "We'll come over when we're finished planting. Love you. See you soon."

"Later," I said and clicked *End.*

Then I pressed his number to reconnect. *I should tell him about the seedlings,* I thought as I watched his number scroll across the screen. But before we connected I pushed *End* again. SOS wouldn't live or die because I went up the mountain or stayed home. Maybe that was the part that hurt so much. Jona cared as much about the environment as I did. He was my perfect replacement, only better.

My positive voice kicked in again. *You're overreacting, Vik. There's no reason the three of you can't be friends. It could be great.* Then my backtalk: *But he's smarter, sexier, and better looking than you, and he likes Linc. What sort of "great" were you thinking about? Are you willing to commit relationship suicide?*

My blood was racing through my veins. Drinking that disgusting coffee only ramped up the shakes. I put my phone on the kitchen table. My hands trembled around the cup. The bottom line was, if Linc chose Jona over me, my life was over.

"What's wrong with you?" Dell gave me her usual warm greeting as she came into the kitchen. She poured the last dregs from the coffee pot into her cup.

"That tastes like crap," I warned her.

She harrumphed and poured sugar from the bottle into her cup. "Why are you here? I thought you were going up the mountain today to save the planet."

"I don't feel well. What about you? I thought you and Bert were going to the rink." If Bert and Dell were planning to stay home, what was already a very bad day had just gotten infinitely worse.

"Can't I get a cup of coffee in my own kitchen without being subjected to your attitude?" she snapped.

"Have as many cups as you want." I got up to leave.

Dell opened her mouth to say something but then bent over and started coughing. When she'd stopped hacking, she said, "Don't talk to me like that, girl. I'm your mother. And don't call your father Bert, either."

Dell was like a drunk, always itching for a fight. She was usually easy to ignore, but I was already agitated and not in the mood to let her get away with taunting me.

"Maybe if he acted like a father I'd call him one."

She sprang out of her chair and lunged at me, her fists raised.

"Leave me alone," I yelled, stepping back. Dell was bigger and tougher than I was. Whenever we had fought in the past, I had gotten the worst of it by a long shot.

Luckily, this time she decided to stop about an arm's length away from me. She put her hand in her pocket and pulled out a cigarette. Then she lit up right in my face.

"God, you're gross. Don't you know mothers are supposed to set a good example for their kids?"

"You can talk, Little Miss Perfect." She took a long drag, curled her tongue, and puffed little smoke rings into the air.

"I guess smoke rings make it stink less?" I said, waving my arms around to disperse the smoke. "I suppose it's better for kids to have cute little curly clouds of smoke filling their lungs?"

"Aren't you a smarty-pants." She squinted as a trail of smoke wound its way around her face. "Just because you quit, that makes you the big judge of the rest of us?"

"Humans are disgusting creatures." I went over and flung open the window. "They destroy everything that's good."

"I thought you were going up the mountain," she said again and flicked her ashes onto the saucer on the counter.

"I'm sick." By then it was true. I had quit smoking when I met Linc, and now second-hand smoke made me retch.

"You don't look sick."

"Shut up, Dell."

"Don't call me that. I'm your mother."

I ran down the hall, slammed my bedroom door behind me, and flopped on the bed.

Dell and Bert weren't parents. Parenting should have something to do with caring and being mature and responsible. On all counts, Dell and Bert didn't qualify.

Jona

"Here's where the ride really gets fun," Linc said as he turned off the highway onto a logging road. It was two bumpy tracks with grass up the middle that scratched the undercarriage of the van. Trees formed a canopy over the road. It felt like we were driving through a tunnel. He'd slowed down, but the van still kept shaking and hitting bottom.

He laughed. "Don't worry. This old van has done this drive dozens of times."

"Has it ever broken down?" I didn't want to sound paranoid, but the thought crossed my mind that we could be stranded for a long time up here before anyone found us.

"A couple of times. The last time, Vik and I just walked back to the highway and hitchhiked home. We used my Uncle Charlie's truck to tow the van out."

I wasn't worried about the van or even about having to walk back to the highway. I wanted to ask about bears and cougars. But I thought I'd save those questions for later.

The landscape was pretty much what I had expected. I'd seen enough pictures to know what replanted cutblocks looked like—sort of. But I had no idea what it would feel like. It wasn't just the idea of running into bears or cougars. It was more like Hansel and Gretel. Not the lost part, but the part about getting swallowed up by the forest. Or was that a different story?

"Wow, this sure isn't Vancouver," I said.

"Maybe Vancouver a couple hundred years ago."

Linc was right. I'd read books about Vancouver in the nineteenth century, when it was nothing but a clear-cut. They were piling the logs on train cars and burning huge piles of slash, and the place looked like a freaking disaster zone.

The forest we were driving through was a strange kind of paradox. There was a weird, messed-up, post-logged-out beauty going on in some places, mossy trees with meadow-like fern gardens underneath. Then, right beside them, were lakes, filled with old snags and stagnant water, that seemed so dead they made me feel sick. The road got dark as we drove through stands of plantation trees that looked like tall crops of corn ready for harvest. A sign showed the name of the logging company and the year the trees had been planted.

"Agricultural forestry," I said. "Every tree is the same size and variety." It was one thing to read about this stuff and another to see it for myself. "I didn't expect it to look this bad."

"At least there are trees. Right?"

Maybe, but it didn't feel good. My brain was throwing questions back and forth like hardballs. I felt hope and doom at the same time. Tree plantations? Really? Was that the best we could do?

After half an hour, the forest stopped and we crossed into what looked like a nuclear bomb site. Huge piles of broken trees were stacked everywhere. They were weathered and grey, like they'd been there for years. The only green came from little alien-looking trees that had sprung up around the piles, but they looked as if they'd eaten something that stunted and deformed them.

"I wish the guy who made this mess was rotting in prison somewhere," I said. "How can a person do this to the land? It's murder." I swallowed the lump in my throat the best I could, but there was no way to stop my eyes from filling with tears. "Didn't anyone remember that bears and deer and beetles and a million other things called this mountain home? This is total annihilation."

"You're just like Vik on our first date," Linc said.

Whoa. I hadn't seen that one coming. Awkward. Super awkward. Maybe he had intended it to sound friendly, not intimate, but it was too late. My emotions were spinning everywhere and I couldn't reel them in. I pressed my fists into my lap and tried to ease the mounting pressure in my groin.

Linc was looking out the window. "You never get over it, but you'll get used to it, like us. Especially once you start to fix it up."

I worked to keep my mind on the conversation. "I'm trying to imagine what it looked like before. I mean, when it was a forest. A real forest. Not just a crop of trees. It must have been super beautiful."

"I know. But it's going to be all good again."

Was he kidding? Could anyone be that positive and be serious?

"Ian, the biologist who's helping SOS, says that forests don't stand still. There's always a ton of life happening, and it'll take off one way or another. Our job is to clean up one stream at a time to get the fish back and give the ecosystem some help. And Vik's been in touch with other groups from all over the place doing work just like SOS."

I wished I could believe him. But "all good"? *Not in our lifetime,* I thought.

"We're making nature's job way too hard," I said. "It can't keep up with how ignorant we are."

"I don't like getting depressed about it. That's not going to do any good. So I try to stay positive. I look at it this way: my work up the hill is like my prayer. Not like a churchy prayer—that's not what I mean. I just know the ancestors are happy that we're doing the work. It's how I can talk to them. And they're happy with Vik for getting it all started."

I'd never thought about such a thing: the ancestors were happy with us. How would that work? Were there crowds of invisible people hanging around? That was intense.

The road had gotten narrower, like the photos I'd seen in books. Shit! It started winding up the side of a hill, and I felt like we were hanging over the cliff. Linc was dodging giant holes, but the van was bottoming out more than ever.

"We'll make it," Linc said, with such confidence I decided I'd just believe him. It was better than freaking out.

"I can't believe I spent so much time in the library learning about this stuff, but I don't know a thing."

"No way, bro. SOS is all heart and a lot of muscle. We need someone like you who's got the brains for it."

Other than taking care of Mom, which I admit I'd done a crappy job of, I was your regular, unremarkable, useless teenager. I had dreams to play music, but in the big picture, let's be serious, the world didn't really need me. Could this ugly-ass mountain be the place where I figured out what the hell I was going to do with my life? Could Linc be right about university or a career? Could I put all that reading to good use?

The treeline jogged to the south, making a weird geometric cut-out shape in the hill.

"Over there," Linc said. I could see the stream up ahead.

We drove down into a gully, and Linc stopped the van and turned off the engine.

He nodded in the direction of an old pickup truck. "Leon's."

We jumped out. I took a couple of long whiffs of air and stretched, which did wonders for my churning stomach. We dragged a couple of totes out of the back of Linc's van and started down a trail that wound through the rubble. Could a few hundred people, or even a thousand, clean up such a mess? In a hundred years?

Where the trail opened out into a clearing at the bank of the stream, Linc dropped his tote and threw his arm around my shoulder. He was almost a head taller than me, and I had never imagined such a feeling. I wanted to grab him and wrestle him to the ground. I knew it was a guy thing that I'd never be able to pull off, but I wasn't sure what I was supposed to do next.

"Over this way." He let his arm drop and moved toward the bank. "Look." He pointed upstream. "The water is running."

This stream didn't look like the murky waterholes we had passed. There were no dead trees in the water. The stream bubbled around riffles and rocks, and the bottom sparkled through the clear water.

"This is it." He raised his hands and waved them in both directions. "It's not a big stretch, but this spot was the major obstruction. Since our work, the stream is flowing smoothly again."

Linc was right to feel good about this. It was like an oasis in the middle of a desert, or a park in the centre of urban chaos. He rocked back on his heels and looked around. "Ian says the stream is coming alive already."

We were standing there, admiring it, when Leon showed up. His pants were soaking wet. "Where were you guys?"

"Sorry, man. I slept in," Linc told him. "But we're here now."

"Slept in? Today?" Leon sounded surprised. "Where's Vik?"

"She didn't come."

"What do you mean? What happened?"

"Nothing happened. She just doesn't feel well."

Leon's surprise turned to concern. "Huh, she sure must be sick to miss this. Ian was asking where she was when he was here earlier. But he had to get going, so he told us everything we need to know about planting the seedlings. He left us the shovels and bags, and, let me tell you, I've got it down." Leon was pumping his muscles. "Now it's up to me, Ian said to tell you. So get ready for an awesome lesson in tree planting."

Leon looked happy that he'd been given the job.

"Everyone else heard Ian's demonstration already. He said we all could get a job planting next year, we were so good," he said with a wide grin. "Billy and I have been hauling the last of the small stuff out of the stream up at the twist. We've just about finished."

"Nice work."

I left Linc and Leon to discuss tree planting and made my way back to nose around the work camp where we had dropped the totes. There was a firepit made out of smooth river stones, and some benches and a table that had been rough cut out of logs. The clearing was encircled by a frame made of branches and covered with plastic that was tied in the corners. Rough-cut shelves held cans of beans and chili, and there was a place for dishes and cutlery and pots and pans.

I was unpacking the totes when Ashley and Ruby showed up.

"Wow," Ruby said. "A man in the kitchen." She nudged me with an empty cup. "You making coffee?"

"I wouldn't be much good at it. For me, making coffee means putting my money down on the counter at Tim Hortons."

She dug around in Linc's tote and produced two large flasks and a plastic container filled with muffins.

"Auntie never fails," she said, eyeing the muffins. Then she got mugs off the shelves for everyone and poured coffee. "Yummm! Anyone besides me want a blackberry muffin?" She ate the top off one while she passed the container to Ashley and me.

I sat on a bench and rested my elbows on the table. No wonder Vik wanted to live up here. Who wouldn't? In my wildest dreams I could never have made up something like this.

After a few minutes, Billy appeared from up the stream, soaking wet. He was barefoot and wore only a pair of cut-offs and a bandanna tied around his head. And, talk about a dream, he looked like an ad for manly deodorant. Impressive. The boy was almost naked and, as far as I could see, didn't have a goosebump. *My God,* I thought, *what is he made of? Steel?*

He sat on the ground, and Ashley hurried over to him with a cup of coffee. She kneeled behind him and started rubbing his shoulders.

"Where's my muffin?" he demanded.

Leon and Linc had joined us by this time.

"God, why don't you two get a room?" Leon said.

Billy ignored Ashley's massage. "Where's my muffin?" he repeated.

"Get your own muffin," Leon told him. "Since when do you have a slave?"

But Ashley had already jumped up to snatch a muffin from the table. Billy stuffed half of it in his mouth, then slapped Ashley's butt and laughed. "She's not my slave," he said, chomping away. "She's my woman."

Ruby spoke up. "Don't take that from him, Ash."

Billy scowled at her. "Hey, baby, pass me a beer," he said to Ashley, pointing to a case on the shelf.

"Get it yourself," she told him. She made it sound like she was joking, but she didn't move.

"That a girl, Ash," Linc said. "I was hoping rednecks like you had gone extinct, like the dinosaurs." He was looking at Billy.

"Shut up." Billy laughed uncomfortably. "Lay off my personal life. We have work to do."

He got himself a beer, flipped the cap, took a long swallow, and let out a loud belch.

"Some of us were here on time this morning." Billy shot an angry look my way. He was standing close enough that I could see his muscles tensing. "We got the how-to from Ian on planting. Now where the hell are the seedlings?"

"The man is right," Leon said. "Billy and I already looked around, and we couldn't find them."

Linc looked at me, then shook his head in frustration.

"Where the hell is Vik, anyways?" Billy asked. "Wasn't this her thing? She was supposed to deal with Ian and find out from the delivery guy where he left the seedlings."

"She's not feeling well," Linc said sharply. "She must have forgotten to call the guy."

"She looked fine last night." Billy took another gulp of his beer. "And then drops us like a hot potato this morning. What's with that?"

"C'mon, Billy," Ashley said. "She must feel like death if she's missing today."

Billy ignored her. "Oh, poor Vik. Now she's got a headache and we don't have the seedlings. That's just fucking beautiful. She's lucky Leon's got the know-how on planting the trees or you guys would be shit out of luck."

"Don't worry, Billy, I got it under control," Leon said.

I felt like telling Billy to shut up, but there was something scary about him. And I was already pretty sure that I wasn't his favourite guy, so I didn't want to get even more on his bad side.

"Yeah, cousin," Ruby said to Billy with no fear in her voice. "You've got it exactly right. Vik's sick and we don't have the seedlings. I don't see any point getting all pissy about it. We just have to find them."

"Why not give her a call?" I said. It was such an obvious solution I wondered why no one else had thought of it.

Everyone broke into fits of laughter.

"Way to go, city boy, except that cell phone companies don't know this place exists," Billy snickered. "Sort of like the rest of the world."

I dug my cell phone out of my pocket. *No service.* This really *was* another planet. What about emergencies, like, for instance, what if someone broke his leg? Or had a heart attack? Or got chewed by a bear? My list of disastrous things that could happen got a mile long in a couple of seconds. There wasn't much I could say without looking like a wimp, though, so I kept my mouth shut.

"There are five cartons of seedlings somewhere up in them there hills," Ashley said in a singsongy voice. She spread her arms out and twirled around. Her hair floated in ringlets as she danced, like a nymph. *The girl of Chutlow Stream,* I thought. I glanced over at Billy. He was still frowning. Was she trying to dance herself back into his good graces? "But the magic place where those cartons are sitting is anybody's guess," she continued.

"We've only got about an hour of work left at the twist," Billy said. He turned away from Ashley. "If no one finds the seedlings by then, I'm going home."

"Ashley and I need to pull the rest of the broom and drag it to the truck," Ruby said. "And then, without the seedlings, there's not much else for us to do either."

At this rate, the day would be over before it got started.

"How about I look for the seedlings?" I said. "I don't know my way around, so I'm thinking that gives me an edge." Probably a really stupid suggestion, but I wanted to stay up the mountain for as long as I could.

Billy frowned at me, then sneered. "Whatever you say, bro. You're apparently the expert. Let's see if all those books you've read will help you get around out here."

Was he making fun of me? Or joking?

Ruby gave me a high-five, though. "Good on you, Jona. You want me to come with you?"

"No. You have work to do. This is a way for me to be useful. At least, it might be."

"Okay, just holler if you get lost," Ruby said. "We'll come and find you."

"Stay out of the woods," Linc said, pointing to the treeline. "Seriously. You could get lost. There's no way the guy dropped the cartons in the woods anyway. He knows what we're doing up here."

Since I was playing the hero, I wasn't going to admit that

Linc had nothing to worry about. There wasn't a chance in hell I would do something stupid. I was too chickenshit to take any kind of physical risk. I started back up the trail the way we had come in.

Ashley yelled after me, "Careful, city boy. We don't want to spend the rest of the day looking for your sorry urban ass."

"Wait," Leon said. He ran up the path behind me and handed me a whistle. "Just in case."

Jesus.

He turned and headed back toward the stream. "Whistle if you're lost," he yelled over his shoulder. "Or if you see a bear."

I brought the whistle up to my mouth, took a breath, and instantly identified a problem. If I saw a bear, I'd be too scared to breathe, let alone blow. What good would a whistle be then? Still, I stuck it in my mouth and did a test run. It made a quiet, squeaky sound. There was some comfort knowing it worked. I looped the cord around my neck and continued up the path. Shit. What if I saw a cougar instead? Was I supposed to blow the whistle then, or play dead?

Seedlings, I said to myself sternly. *That is the task at hand.* Task, or ridiculous proposition? If Billy and Leon couldn't find them, why the hell did I think I could? I went to the place in my head I always did when things seemed impossible—logic. Logic reduced the element of chaos and, if things went well, could turn the situation into something manageable. Even if I was being delusional, being logically delusional was preferable to being randomly delusional.

I started from the premise that the driver actually took the right logging road. If he didn't, the seedlings would be on some other miscellaneous mountain and were as good as dead.

The next logical question: Where would a delivery guy drop a bunch of cartons? I walked off the trail and along a gully toward the treeline. The trouble was, the driver could have been thinking about the hockey game or where he was going for lunch or screwing his girlfriend. How was I to know? Maybe he was doing a favour for a friend and didn't know where the hell he was. Or he might have dumped the cartons any-freaking-where because he was late for a dentist appointment.

I looked around. The place was a disaster zone. There was not one logical thing about it. I realized that if I was going to find the seedlings, I'd have to abandon logic and try something else. My body started to rattle until I could hear my teeth chatter.

I kept walking until my shirt was damp and I was calm enough that all I could hear was the sound of my own breathing. Off to the right was a grassy spot, open and flat. It seemed like the kind of place a guy would drop some cartons of baby trees, but it was obvious there was nothing there. With the bald face of the mountain rising above me, I flung my arms out sideways and began to turn like those crazy-looking monk guys who spin and spin and spin. A weird giggle spiralled out of me and I fell backwards, thrashing my hands and feet. I was a little kid throwing a tantrum. Insanity had invaded my sweaty body. Every gob-stopping emotion I had stuffed in my veins busted loose into the chaos of that clear-cut. I was high, hysterical, soaring higher and higher.

Bits of my brain told me to stop, but there was no chance of it. My exhilaration had taken on a life of its own. Jesus, what if I never stopped?

I flopped around on my back like a beached fish. It took a

while for the madness to peter out, and I watched the clouds chasing each other while a flock of crows played in the wind. As I listened to their caws, I wondered what they were saying about the mess that had been made of this place and the crazy kid spazzing out on the ground.

The air tingled as it seeped into my lungs. Cool oxygen fed my blood as it rushed through my body. I was alive.

Slowly I got up and shook the twigs off my back and out of my hair. I checked around to make sure no one had seen me.

I emerged from the gully back onto the road and crossed to the other side. *Why did the city kid cross the logging road?* It sounded like the opening of a terrible joke. Then, right across from the place where I'd lost my mind, there they were. Five cardboard boxes, each big enough to hold a small TV, were stacked in front of me. The words *VICTORIA BUCKINGHAM* were scrawled in black felt pen on the top and sides.

I climbed onto a pile of logs and faced downhill toward the stream. I blew the whistle and waved my arms. "Over here. Whoo hooooo," I hollered at the top of my lungs. "Seedlings found. Whooo, whoooo, whoooo."

After a few minutes I saw Linc's and Billy's heads bobbing among the rubble. I scrambled to the highest point of the pile and wobbled until I got my balance. Like a screaming maniac, I let loose again. "Over here. Over here." I couldn't stop chanting the words, even when Billy and Linc got there.

They looked up at me, laughing their heads off. Billy shouted, "You are a fucking idiot."

"I'm an idiot? What does that make this?" I swung around, almost knocking myself off my perch. "Check out the scene, bro. We are looking at utter stupidity."

Billy climbed up the pile and did his own balancing act on the log next to me. He beat his chest until it sounded like a drum and he was looking like a scene out of an old cowboys and Indians movie. But then he started hollering a chant. The sound was coming out of the pit of his stomach. *This is real,* I thought. It had a rhythm so guttural it gave me goosebumps.

By the time we climbed down, Linc had hauled the cartons out onto the road. “How did you find them all the way up here?”

“Sheer, blind luck,” I confessed. “I had just about given up and then I almost stubbed my toe on them.”

We took one carton each and headed back down the path.

Ashley cheered as we arrived at the camp. Ruby ran over and threw her arms around me. “A hero’s welcome for Jona.” She kissed my cheek.

“Hold on,” Ashley said. She clicked a few photos with her cell. “I’m gonna post these later.”

Billy jumped in behind us. “Come on, take it, take it. I carried one of the damn things back here.” Linc joined in too, wrapping his arms around us.

“Good shot,” Ashley said. “I’m going to call it the Great Seedling Rescue.”

“Thank you,” I said, with a little bow. “Come on, Billy, let’s go get the other two cartons.”

By the time we returned, Linc had opened the cartons and laid the seedling trays on the ground. There were red alder, yellow cedar, pine, fir, big-leaf maple, native crabapple, thimbleberry, salmonberry, and willow.

“Everyone gets a bag,” Leon said as he began filling each one, “with the species divided in them. They aren’t light once they're full, so be careful you don't kill your back. Ian said when we get good at planting, we can really load them up.

"Ian divided the area out into plots," he continued. "Linc, we figured you and Jona could do the area upstream by the pool."

Leon demonstrated how to hold a shovel in our right hand and take the trees from the bag with our left. Then he showed us how to space the plants so they wouldn't compete with each other for light when they began to grow.

"You have to plant them at exactly the right depth," he said. "Not too deep. Ian said the seedling's roots need to be flush with the ground."

Using the shovel, he showed us how to dig a proper-sized hole. He grabbed a tree from his bag, and in the same fluid motion, like a pro, he bent over and plopped the tree into the hole. Then he used his right foot to kick the hole closed. He pointed to the seedling. "No air gaps," he said, "or the root will dry out."

He stood up and grinned. "Expert or what?"

"Holy shit, you're good," I said. "I've read about tree planting, but you make it look like pure music."

"Ian said this is how regular tree planters plant out the cutblocks, although they are mainly putting in only pine and spruce. We're using varied species to replant the riparian zone along the stream the way it should be done." He pulled a paper out of his pocket. "He gave me this and said everyone who's planting needs to hear it so they understand what we're doing." He read, "*Each species has a place in the ecosystem. The willow and the alder grow quickly and stabilize the stream bank. The maple accumulates minerals in its leaves, and when they drop in the fall it feeds the soil. The crabapples and berries feed the animals, which then also fertilize the soil with their droppings.*"

"Wow, thanks," Linc said. "That's great to know."

I'd read almost the same thing, sitting in the Vancouver library. Now, though, it seemed like it was written in a different language. One that I could really understand.

"Now you guys are on your own," Leon said and headed off down the trail. "Ruby and I have a plot of our own to plant."

Linc and I started planting side by side. "This is incredible," I said to him. "We are actually creating an ecosystem, so different from the rows of trees we saw in the cutblocks on the way up."

Leon was right: the bag was damn heavy, though Linc made it look like it was light as a feather. I struggled to match his pace, move for move, but he was like a tree-planting machine. I felt good in spite of the fact that my back and legs were yelling at me, while Linc had hardly broken a sweat. In less than an hour, the planting was done.

"I need to get out more," I gasped. "City life and libraries didn't prepare me for this kind of work."

"It won't take long before you're a full bushwhacker." He laughed and threw his bag and shovel on the ground.

I collapsed on a stump. Pain shot through every muscle of my body. Linc hooked his butt on the stump, close enough for me to feel his body heat, and his musky scent made me forget my aches and pains.

Two perfect rainbows arched over the mountain to one side of us. The sky behind them was dark, as if a storm was brewing, but in the other direction the sun shone in a blue sky.

"I thought you were too much of a city kid to get your hands dirty."

"Me too. I didn't know I had it in me. I've always made sure

I recycle coffee cups and pop cans and plastic cutlery," I said. "I felt like I was doing the environment a big freaking favour. But really I was doing nothing at all."

"I don't know," Linc said. "I think every little bit helps."

He pointed at the deepest part of the stream. It was the size of a couple of large hot tubs.

"Last one in the water buys coffee."

"Are you out of your mind?" I needed a real hot tub, not a dunk in freezing water.

"Absolutely serious. On the count of three."

He stood up and stripped off his T-shirt. "One." He kicked off his boots, unzipped his jeans, and started sliding them over his butt.

"No way, man," I said, starting to freak. "Don't make me do it."

"Come on, chickenshit."

I was searching for a way to be fine with being chickenshit this time. It was better than freezing my ass off. But worse than that, I didn't want to strip down to my boxers. Not next to Linc. He was stretching and flexing and bouncing on the balls of his feet. He looked like a prizefighter.

"But think of all the damage we'll do to the newly revived ecosystem," I said.

"Our people have been bathing in streams since forever. The fish haven't seemed to mind."

I knew I had no choice. "Okay. Okay." The quicker I got it over with, the better.

I ripped off my jacket and pulled my shirt over my head. A blast of cold air hit my chest. God, what a stupid thing to do. I kicked off my shoes and stepped out of my jeans. Once my socks were off and I was standing with my skinny legs dangling out of my boxer shorts, I sucked in one big breath and took off like a shot, right past Linc.

Quick freeze. I couldn't freaking breathe. It felt like I was being attacked by a million tiny glass arrows.

Linc landed in the water and sent a freezing wave over my head.

All I could do was squeak out "Coffee's on you."

"Holy, you're fast." He hitched his butt up onto a rock in the water and lounged back in the pool as if it really were a hot tub.

Covered in mountainous goosebumps, I clambered out of the water and up the bank. "The last time I was this cold..." My teeth chattered so hard I almost bit my tongue. "What do I mean? I've *never* been this cold."

"We'll toughen you up," Linc said, moving slowly as he climbed out. "Pretty soon you'll be begging for a dunk in the stream."

I rubbed myself down with my jacket and tugged on my clothes. "I doubt that." I still couldn't keep my jaw steady. "My body doesn't know what hit it." I handed him my jacket to dry off. "No point killing two good jackets for this."

I tried to avoid staring, but how can you help watching a scene like that? How could genetics get everything so right at one time to produce such a specimen? I wanted to get a few shots of him with my phone, but it didn't seem right.

I was probably still gaping when Billy and Ashley showed up.

"Way to go, Jona. You took the dive," she said. "You'll be a real west coaster soon." She brushed past Linc, unfazed by the awesome display of his body.

"What kind of west coasters are you guys?" Linc challenged. "I don't see you jumping in."

"Next time," Billy said. "I'm looking for a cold beer, not a cold pond."

I walked a couple of steps behind them on the way back to camp, trying to take in the whole scene. Had today actually happened? It was as if someone had lit a match under me. Every cell in my body was fired up and ready to go.

Vik

To keep Dell out of my face, I'd locked my bedroom door. I set the pillows up on the bed for a backrest, plugged in my earbuds, and climbed onto the bed, then covered my legs with my favourite kid blanket. On a normal day, wrapping myself in my "blankie" would have put me in my super comfort zone. But today wasn't normal.

I pulled my knitting out of the basket and tried to concentrate on the infinity scarf I was making, without thinking about anything else. I was on the simple part, where I only needed to change colours to make cool bold stripes. It was easy—there was no chance for anything to go wrong. I'd taught myself to knit from the Internet when I was about twelve, and now I was good enough I could almost do it with my eyes closed. Throw the wool around the needle and pass it off, throw the wool around the needle and pass it off. I gave the yarn a little tug after each stitch to keep it taut, so that every one was an exact replica of the one before, and each row lined up perfectly. Knitting is the ideal activity for obsessives. You can repeat the same action over and over and demand absolute perfection, and no one else will know.

I checked my phone: ten fifty-six. I measured my knitting. Two inches in one hour...twenty-four inches to go and the scarf would be finished. I took my earbuds out and listened. The house was silent. I opened my bedroom door, and the echoey creak of the hinges gave off a hollow no-one's-home feel. A note from Dell leaned up against the ketchup squirter on the kitchen table. *GONE TO THE BONSPIEL. BACK LATE.*

The thick black letters made me feel like she wanted to continue our fight. But she'd added a happy face in the bottom corner. Which, I guessed, was meant to make up for everything. Or maybe it was meant to confuse me. How was I to know? That was Dell all over. Underneath, Bert had scrawled *Stay home today.*

Even his writing made me cringe. How could a man turn out like Bert? Did something horrible happen to him when he was a kid that twisted his brain? One thing I *did* know: having a daughter was not his idea. I was only five the first time I realized Bert and I would never get along. He and Dell were having one of their yelling matches in the living room. I was in bed with my hands over my ears, but I could still hear the thud of his fist against her body. Dell screeched with pain, and then I heard her whimpering. I snuck out of my room and down the hall. Bert's back blocked me from seeing everything, but his arm was raised, with his hand clenched in a fist. Dell crouched on the floor in front of him. I was confused, since it looked like she was praying.

"I never wanted that fucking little bastard," he hollered. "And now look at me. I'm stuck with her and you."

"She's your daughter," Dell sobbed.

He drew his foot back, and I squeezed my eyes shut so I wouldn't have to see him kick her. I didn't remember anything else except that my pajama pants had been wet when I climbed back into bed, and I lay there freezing all night, afraid to move.

I threw the old coffee grinds into the compost and put on a fresh pot. I made toast and carried my breakfast into the living room. It felt eerie. When was the last time I had hung out here? Years ago. Ever since the mill closed and Bert lost his job, the living room had been his domain 24-7, and I stayed out of there as much as I could.

I stood at the front window and slurped my coffee. *Mmmm... better than the first cup.*

I could almost hear Bert saying, *Vik! If you're going to drink like a horse, do it outside.*

I slurped again, louder this time. Then I slurped the longest slurp I could without gagging. I laughed out loud, thinking about how much he would hate it.

Shards of sunlight shot into the room and warmed the skin on my face. Soon my momentary feeling of freedom was replaced with the wish that I had gone up the mountain.

It's too late, I reminded myself. *You made your decision. Stop being so pitiful. You are home for the day. Just be thankful Bert and Dell are out.*

Trying to make my self-talk positive was hard to do this morning. No matter how I tried to derail the train, all I could think about was Linc and Jona. From what I'd read on the Internet, I wasn't full-blown OCD. I wasn't obsessive about brushing my teeth with exactly fifty-two strokes or anything like that. But I needed things to be organized, and I got agitated when they weren't. And I guess I liked counting things, like seconds and minutes when I ran, and stitches and rows when I knitted. But I wasn't a total control freak. At least, I didn't think I was. But I had to admit that I was frantic to make the world a better place. Was that OCD, though, or just sensible? And now

I couldn't let go of the idea that Jona was stealing Linc right out from under my nose. I had no idea if it was sensible or not, but I knew that it was making me crazy.

I set my cup and plate on the coffee table and curled up on the sofa, wrapping the afghan around my shoulders. It was one of Dell's ugly second-hand finds, crocheted in green and gold granny squares. I examined the stitches and liked the way wear and tear had pulled every stitch evenly tight. But what was it about crochet that made it look so much harder than knitting?

Our living room was the kind of place the Reno Man would use for a "before" shot on one of his total-makeover shows. He'd call the décor Early Walmart or Bad Garage Sale. The walls were covered with plaques and hangings spouting every platitude in the book. *Home is where the heart is. Patience is a virtue. Just follow your heart. Look on the bright side.* If you didn't know better, you would have thought we were the ultimate happy family.

Over the fireplace was a black velvet painting of a biker on a motorcycle, a woman in short shorts cozied up behind him. Underneath it, the plaque read *You are not alone. Angels are by your side.* I cringed. What had Linc thought of it the first time he came over here? What would Jona say if he saw it? My cheeks got hot.

I shut my eyes before the room could swallow me up. Who would decorate a room like this? Bert and Dell, that's who. I felt like an alien. *When Linc and I get a place,* I thought, *it's not going to look like this.*

But what if I don't get out of here soon enough, and I turn out like them?

I wanted to rip the stupid plaques off the walls and chuck

them in the dump. *Dell and Bert might be your biology,* I reminded myself, *but they aren't your destiny. In a year and a half you will be out of the house. You and Linc will be at university—together. Goodbye, Carterton. You will be free.*

But the negative voice wouldn't let me jump the tracks. *Don't be so sure. Jona is angling his way in, and he's going to mess you up.* Hard as I tried, I couldn't feel positive.

I burst into tears. "No. No. No. No." A few minutes of deep breathing—in, one two three four, and out, one two three four—got me off the couch at least. I went back into the kitchen and put my dishes in the sink. I caught a look at myself in the mirror hanging by the door and did a few selfie poses. When I parted my lips, they turned up more on the left side than the right. My top lip was thin. My bottom lip was full and pouty. It was Dell's mouth—exactly. There was nothing really wrong with it. But how could I like a mouth that was the same as hers?

"Victoria Buckingham." I moved my lips deliberately with each syllable, thinking about the one and only time Grandma Beryl had phoned from England to talk to me. I was about eight, and it was just a few years before she died. I'd never forgotten what she told me.

"As long as you remember your name, my precious girl, you will remember where you are from." Her words dripped with a syrupy English accent. Her call was a lifeline. It reminded me, as I stood in the middle of our tacky house, that I wasn't trailer trash and that I didn't belong there with Bert and Dell. I was Victoria Buckingham, with a family that was rich and important on the other side of the world.

Dell never said much about her family, but I knew I'd been

named after England's Queen Victoria. She was supposed to be a distant relation, a great-great-aunt twice removed or something. Sometimes I wondered if it was just a giant BS story, cooked up because Grandma Beryl and Dell's last name was Buckingham and mine was too. By some miracle, Dell had convinced Bert to let me have her name, not his. At least, that was her story. For all I knew, he wouldn't let me take his name. Either way, I was glad to be Victoria Buckingham and not Victoria Fromski.

Even if I didn't believe the story about royal relatives, I knew Grandma Beryl, if she hadn't died, would have been there for me. And there was actual proof we were related to rich people. A ring. Sitting in Bert and Dell's bedroom.

Since the first time I saw it, I had made many plans to sneak another look, maybe touch it, but each time I chickened out. My heart pounded at the idea—I wanted that proof in my hand. I needed to know that I was more than Bert and Dell.

Now, just like every other time, I started to get nervous. It felt like someone was inside my head, listening to my thoughts, or like there were hidden cameras around the house spying on me.

"Anyone home?" I called. How stupid did that sound? "Dell? Bert? Are you here?"

I went into the kitchen and reread Dell's note. *Gone to the bonspiel. Back late.* I read it several times. A bonspiel meant they wouldn't be home until midnight. That gave me lots of time to go through with my plan. They'd never know.

I walked down the hall and stopped in front of Dell and Bert's room. I couldn't stop myself from glancing over my shoulder. It was as if imaginary eyes were boring holes in my back. *Are you losing it, Vik? Just go in there,* I told myself. I took some deep breaths—in, one two three four, and out, one two three four. I wiped my sweaty hands on the seat of my jeans, twisted the knob, opened the door, and stepped inside.

Their room was strictly out of bounds. I'd only been in there a couple of times when I was a kid. Even the thought of entering the room made Bert's voice sound in my head: *"I'll wring your neck"* and *"I'll smack you to kingdom come if you so much as step foot in there."* But now, here I was.

Lavender paint covered all four walls of the bedroom as well as the ceiling and window frames. Dell's favourite colour. The pink and orange floral bedspread still clashed with the lavender, but not as badly as it did before. The sun had faded everything.

The last time I was in this room, I had been about ten. "Come on," Dell had urged in a whisper. Bert was at work, but her eyes darted from side to side, as if he was going to jump out and attack us. I liked the feeling of our forbidden adventure. We were robbers or trespassers, though I had no idea what Dell was up to.

She opened the top drawer of her dresser and pulled out a key. Then she unlocked the blanket box at the end of the bed and rummaged around in the folded linens until she retrieved a beautiful wooden box. She sat down on the bed and put the box on her lap. I stood gaping at it, as if she had found buried treasure. "Sit down," she said to me. The box was made of a dark wood with lines of buttery coloured wood along the sides. She stroked the mosaic design of exotic birds inlaid on the lid. "This is mother-of-pearl," she told me, keeping her voice low. "Bert bought this for me."

Then she said, "Never come in here, Vik. Bert would kill you." Although I'd heard his threats many times by then. "And don't ever tell him about what we've done today. He'd kill me."

I held my breath as she opened the lid a crack at a time, until the tinkling sound of music filled the room. I was mesmerized. It sounded like rich people's music, and even then I couldn't imagine Bert buying such a thing.

Now, years later, I repeated Dell's actions exactly. I found the key in the top drawer of the dresser and opened the blanket box, setting the key on top of the dresser as I lifted the lid. I buried my hands in the folded linens until I felt the hard corners of the jewellery box.

It was smaller than I remembered, and it looked more like something Dell had found at the second-hand store than an exotic treasure. I lifted the lid slowly—expecting with each tiny crack to hear the tinkling sound of Beethoven or Mozart, but when I had opened the lid wide, the box was silent.

The same drugstore-style jewellery was piled in the top section of the box. I pulled on the tabs at either end to lift the top tray out and put it on the dresser. In the bottom of the box was the faded yellow newspaper clipping and the bundle of green velvet tied with a white satin ribbon.

I picked up the clipping first and unfolded it on my lap. Across the top ran the words *Birmingham Daily Post.* Underneath was a photo that took up almost half the page and a caption: "*Beryl Buckingham, Queen of the May, Napton on the Hill, wins the 1956 Midlands Beauty Contest.*"

Grandma Beryl, in movie-star splendour, was sitting up on the back of a long sleek convertible driven by a man in a tuxedo, a top hat, and white gloves. She had tightly curled blonde hair and dark lipstick. Her tiny waist was accentuated by pointed breasts that looked like they were encased in armour.

How could a girl with such elegance and sophistication have

been my grandmother? I looked closely at her facial features, at her thin top lip and pouty bottom lip for reassurance. Her smile turned up on the left side just a little higher than on the right, and her eyes drooped slightly at the edges, exactly like mine.

I might not have been as beautiful as Grandma, and I didn't have a drop of her glamour, but I was still her granddaughter. "*As long as you remember your name, my precious girl, you will remember where you are from.*"

In the photo she held a rose in one hand and was giving the Queen's wave with the other. And on her middle finger, on the hand she held in the air, was a ring with a stone the size of a marble.

I folded the picture carefully and put it back in the box. Then I picked up the green velvet bundle. I laid it on my lap and untied the ribbon. Slowly I unfolded the corners of the velvet. There, in the centre of the cloth, lay Grandma's ring. The gold band looked hardly strong enough to hold the enormous mound of stones. A huge emerald, cut in the shape of a teardrop, was surrounded by what looked like dozens of diamonds. I counted them. Twenty-six.

I shifted my knees a little to angle the emerald into the sun and watched the light sparkle off the stone.

I could hear Dell's and Bert's warnings ringing in my brain. But it didn't matter. I imagined what Grandma Beryl would have been saying to me if she was still alive. "*You're not meant to be living in that pathetic place with that horrible man who calls himself your father. You are a Buckingham. This ring is for you. Put it on your finger, my precious girl.*"

Linc

"Sure you don't want to stick around for some canned chili?" Ashley asked.

She was making a fire in the kitchen up on the mountain, and Billy was sitting at the table, about to crack another beer.

"I gotta get going," I said.

"You should wait and hike upstream with Leon and me," Ruby said. "We're going to look for bear tracks."

"Thanks anyway. I want to get home. I need to phone Vik to see how she's feeling."

"Tell her we missed her," Ruby said. She threw me a few kisses. "Those are for her."

"From me too," Ashley said. She kissed her fingers and flickered them in the air.

Billy flipped his chin. "Yeah, tell Vik thanks for screwing us over. Tell her next time she should follow through on what she says."

"Really, Billy?" Ashley looked disgusted. "I can't believe you said that."

"Whatever, Ash. You know it's true. Everyone knows it's true."

"Don't push me, cousin," I said. I wasn't in the mood to fight him, but I couldn't just stand there and take his shit, not when he was slagging Vik.

"Oh, you mean you don't want me pushing you around like she does? Face it, cousin, she's got you wrapped around her little finger." He got up and bumped my arm with his chest.

"Shut up, Billy. You're full of shit," Ruby piped in. "If it weren't for Vik, none of us would be here. And she's my best friend, so quit with the nasty shit."

"You're as bad as Linc," Billy said. "Thinking he's too good for us Indians."

I reached for his arm and yanked him toward me until we were nose to nose. "Shut the fuck up, Billy. I'm no better than you and no worse. Neither is Vik. Once and for all, leave her alone. And me. Or you are going to get hurt."

He tried to shake me off, but I held on long enough to let him know I meant it. When I let him go, he slumped back onto the bench.

Jona and I folded up the empty cardboard cartons so we could pack them back to the van.

"Are you sure you don't want to stick around?" I asked him. "You could catch a ride with Leon."

"Yeah," Ruby said to Jona. "We'll make room for you. C'mon, it's early, and the bears are waiting for you to find them."

Jona laughed. I was happy when he said, "No, thanks. I think I'll head back down with Linc." I needed someone to talk to.

We jumped in the van. "I'm glad to be heading back," I said to Jona. "That's the first time I've ever felt this way when I'm driving down the mountain. It was great today, but it wasn't the same without Vik."

Not only did I miss her, but as soon as I started driving, I got to wondering what she was up to. I needed to get home and straighten things out. "She'll be happy you found the seedlings," I said to Jona.

"It was more like they found me."

I didn't know what to think about him. There was no one like him in Carterton, and I wanted to know more about him, where he'd been and what he thought. I liked listening to him. There just weren't any guys around who had interesting things to say. And he had an eager, little-kid quality about him that made him different.

Jona was sitting up, straight-backed, looking out the window as if he didn't want to miss a thing.

"Where are you from, man?"

"Uh, Vancouver?" he said.

I laughed. "I mean your people. Where are your people from?"

"One half come from miscellaneous European countries. England, Germany, Scotland. The other half are Mohawks from Six Nations in Ontario."

"That's your old man."

"Yeah."

"Where is he?"

He was quiet for a few moments and then said, "Dead."

The word swam around in the van like an old fish. Neither of us wanted to touch the subject.

"Mine too," I said finally. "What happened to yours?" I didn't want to ask him another pushy question, but I really wanted to know.

"Cancer." Jona spat the word out as if it had fangs and a pitchfork. "He died of cancer."

"Mine offed himself before I got a chance to know him," I blurted.

He swung around and looked at me straight on, shocked.

"Mom says he used to love going up to the stream," I said. "Whenever I come up here, I think maybe he died because they killed it."

The words came out of my mouth like I was talking about what I had for breakfast…eggs, hash browns, and fried tomatoes. I sounded like a zombie.

"Brutal. I'm sorry, man." Jona's voice cracked, as if he was holding back tears.

I definitely didn't want him breaking down right there in the car with me, so I said, "I never really knew him." And trying to soften the conversation up a little, I said, "I guess I sort of get to know him when I'm working up here."

The mood in the van still felt heavy, so I shrugged. "Hey, you get what you get. It's not like anyone gives us a choice."

"I guess I'm lucky. If you can call it that. At least I can remember my dad."

"Was he a good guy?"

"Yeah." He paused. "At least, I think so. It's been killing my mom ever since he's been gone. She kind of got stuck there, and, like I told you, until now she hardly ever left the house. But I was only four when he died, so for all I know he was an asshole." He made a weak attempt at laughing.

"I've heard people say that us kids are better off without my old man," I said. "Mom says the world got to be too much for him. I figure that's why she's so hardcore on making sure I'm strong enough to cope. She says if the world gets to be too much, you should kick it in the ass. Ha, that's what she did. She raised three of us. I'm the youngest. Cath's at university and Rob's a dentist, so she's pretty damn proud of herself."

"Good job. My mom could have used her ass-kicking lesson," Jona said. "Mom couldn't even raise me, never mind two other kids. But what people said about your old man…I don't think they're right. I'm pretty sure that we'd both be better off if we had our dads."

"You might be right." But I was already missing him, and it wasn't something I liked to think about much.

I passed Jona my phone. "You want to dial Vik's number as soon as we get to the highway? The signal will be strong enough there, and I need to tell her we're on our way."

Vik

The ring slid over my knuckles easily. I scrunched my baby and middle fingers together to hold the giant cluster of stones in place and put my hand in the sun to watch the light glint off the emerald. It was like a magnet—I couldn't take my eyes off it. But how did Grandma wear it? It was so big.

Bert always talked about how the ring was his ticket out of Carterton and into the good life.

"That damn ring is our retirement plan, Delly, thanks to old Beryl," he would say. "Stingy old broad. If we'd got what we deserved, we'd be sitting pretty right now. The ugly thing is worth ten times as much as this house. Just you wait, Delly, my princess. Once the kid is out of our hair, it's going to be you and me on the beach under a palm tree drinking margaritas."

Dell would play along. She'd dance around him and put on an English accent. God, just thinking about him made me cringe.

The day Dell showed me the ring, she explained that after Grandma Beryl's will was settled, she'd received a package, special delivery.

"It was just a tiny little box," she said. "Bert tore it to shreds trying to get into it. Then, there it was: the green velvet bundle, the newspaper clipping, and a copy of the will. My brother and sister sent us the will to rub it in that they got everything else."

That day, Dell held the velvet cloth but never laid a finger on the ring. It was as if it were contaminated. But I thought it was the most beautiful thing I had ever seen. I imagined I was Cinderella, only it would be the ring that would turn me into the princess I really was.

"What could I expect?" she said as she folded the velvet around the ring and put it back into the jewellery box. "I only talked to your grandma once or twice after I ran away. And she didn't talk to me, either. How was I to know she would up and die on us so soon?"

Being just a kid at the time, I didn't understand. And I wasn't sure I even understood now what would have made Dell choose Bert and Carterton over her family in England.

"If I'd gone back home and married the boy they wanted me to marry," she said, "I'd have been rich too. But if I had to do it again, Vik, I would make the same decision and run as far away from your grandma as I could get. Old Beryl never liked me. I think I came out of the pipe disappointing her. I'm sure she was happy when I ran away." So maybe the ring was all Dell was ever going to get, no matter what.

I held my hand in the light and looked at it closely. How could there be so many diamonds attached around the emerald? How did the delicate band hold so many stones?

I did the Queen's wave. The floral bedspread and lavender walls faded until I was sitting on the back of a convertible with the crowds roaring as I drove past. The ring was my transformer. I was too old now for princess dreams, but the ring was still proof that I was not totally a small-town redneck. I wanted to keep the fantasy alive, and the ring was too magnificent to be stuck in such an ugly room, so, holding my hand carefully by my side, I stood up and walked out of the bedroom, leaving the door slightly ajar. Clenching my fist to keep the ring safe, I put on my coat and stepped out the back door. My heart raced as I thought of the chance I was taking. But as I stood on the porch, I knew exactly where I wanted to go.

Sun still streamed through the clouds in some places, but when I took a deep breath of the heavy, damp air, I made a mental bet that the clouds would win the battle for the skies.

I went down the stairs and tromped through the long grass, past Bert's motorcycle shed and the blackberry vines, to the maple tree and the hedgerow at the far end of what, in a real family, would have been the back lawn. I crouched under the low branches and brushed overgrown vines and prickles out of my way so I could crawl through what had been my secret passageway. I crept a few steps like a crab. There, next to the big oak, almost completely surrounded by hunks of granite, was the soft mossy mound, just like I remembered it.

When I was a kid, I'd moved stones and filled in the cracks with moss to make walls on three sides. I called it my cave. When Bert was angry, he would chase me as far as the hedgerow, then get so furious at his inability to squeeze through that he'd let me go. I would pretend I was a missing kid, like the ones on the milk cartons. I thought that if I stayed out there long enough, Bert and Dell would miss me and worry. I dreamed about the whole neighbourhood gathering at our house and heading out as a search party. I listened for the sound of dogs and people marching through the yard until I was too hungry and cold to believe my fantasy any longer. Eventually, I had to go back into the house, knowing that Bert hadn't forgotten why he had come after me in the first place.

The "cave" felt a lot smaller than I remembered. I stood in the middle of it and looked back at the house. I was tall enough now to see into the kitchen window.

I spread my coat on the cushiony moss, sat down, and raised the ring in the air. I re-examined every detail. I wanted to feel the excitement I always had felt just thinking about the ring, but somehow the more I looked at it, the less I liked it. Out here, the setting looked heavy and overdone, and without the sun the stones lost their shine. It was as if someone had said to a jeweller, "Make me the biggest damn emerald ring in the world. And make sure it has so many diamonds that no one will be able to hold it up."

Grandma Beryl wouldn't have had just this one expensive ring, I thought. *She would have had a whole jewellery box full of them, and expensive clothes and cars and tons of everything else she wanted.*

But what if Grandma Beryl had so much because she and Grandpa Arnold were the kind of rich people George Carter was, not caring what they destroyed as long as they got their money? Bert always said he deserved the ring because Dell's family got rich off poor people. Dell would tell him to shut up, but what if he was right? And, the worst question of all, the one that I'd never let myself ask: Why did Grandma Beryl only call me once? If I was so precious, why hadn't she talked to me more often? Or sent for me to visit her in England?

The whole thing started to give me the creeps. I got to thinking about genetic pools: mine was contaminated on both sides. Being Grandma Beryl's granddaughter didn't feel any better than being Bert Fromski's daughter from Carterton.

The sounds of a breeze rustling through the leaves made

me wish with everything I had that I was up the mountain with Linc. He was the only person who had ever been real family to me. And now I was hiding in my childhood getaway with a bunch of damn ugly stones on my finger, and he was probably having a great time with someone else. *How perfectly pathetic, Vik.*

But, God, I was tired. I hadn't slept for half the night, and the moss was soft and comfortable. I rolled into a ball and closed my eyes. I breathed in, one two three four, and out, one two three four. The wind was getting stiffer in the trees, and far off a raven chortled.

A loud thumping was coming from inside and outside my head. Percussive sounds clattered over a roaring hum. Lines and zigzags shot back and forth before my eyes, and bright splashes of colour spun in circles. Shadows of black bodies lurked around the edges of the scene, gradually creeping closer and closer to the centre. Thrashing and terrified, I tried to identify a menacing voice making eerie attempts to wake me up. I screamed but no sound came out. *Wake up. Just wake up, Vik, and it will all go away.* But I couldn't wake up, either. Then a loud clanging, like a fire alarm, smashed through my horrible dream.

I jumped up, scrambled through the hedgerow, and raced across the lawn. I was on the back porch before I realized it was the house phone ringing. I bolted through the door, grabbed the phone, and dropped onto a kitchen chair. My knees quivered, and my heart pounded so hard I could hear it.

"Hello?"

Linc said, "Hey, babe. You all right?"

"No, not really. I was having an awful dream and then the house phone started ringing and it totally freaked me out."

"Sorry. You didn't answer your cell."

I glanced around and wondered where it was. "I'm not sure where I put it." I shook my head, trying to wake up.

"It was awesome up the mountain. I finished the bank you and I were working on. And Jona found the seedlings. He was the hero of the day."

We haven't been talking for even one minute, and Linc is already gushing about Jona.

"Ian got up there earlier and we missed him. But he showed the others how to plant the seedlings. Leon passed on the instructions to us."

"I hope he's not mad at me."

"Leon?" Linc sounded surprised.

"No, Ian. I hope he didn't mind that I wasn't there."

"Leon said everything was fine. In fact, Leon really got into the instruction thing and looked as if he liked being in charge."

I was honestly relieved that it had all worked out. "Good for him."

"We did it all. Just like you dreamed about, babe. How about we take a drive up there tomorrow so you can check it out? Make sure you approve?"

Is that a dig about me being bossy? Were they talking about me up on the mountain?

"Jona and I even had a dunk in the pool."

I heard Jona yell, "A super ass-freezing dunk."

That was our pool. It was the special place Linc and I went when we were up the mountain. The thought of Linc and Jona in the pool made my head spin.

A loud knock startled me. "Hold on. I gotta get the door."

There was a pause on the phone as I walked down the hall and opened the front door.

"Surprise," Linc said. "I'm here."

He opened his arms, and I collapsed into his embrace. He tightened his grip and lifted me up until my toes couldn't touch the ground. I could feel his heart beating, and for a few seconds I forgot my ugly thoughts about Jona taking my place in the pool.

When he put me down, I saw Jona standing behind him on the steps. His hair was wet. Half of it was hanging in strings, and he was braiding the other half.

"Hey, Vik," Jona said. "Great work you've done up the stream."

I wanted to spit, but I clenched my jaw instead.

Jona carried on. "Today changed my life. Really. I'm serious."

Didn't he get it? I didn't give a shit if he changed into a damn butterfly. I didn't want to hear about it.

"Then, to top it off, Linc forced me into the water." He broke into a grin. I pulled away from Linc. "I froze my ass off, but, holy, I got a high! I can't wait to go back. I totally get why you could live up there. It's freaking magic."

Linc lightly punched his shoulder. "I told you so."

What the hell had they been talking about? *If I have my way you will never go back,* I screamed inside. *First my seat in the van and now my place in the pool. No. No. No. Can it get any worse?*

"When will Dell and Bert be home?" Linc asked.

"They're at a bonspiel, so not until late tonight."

Linc stepped inside the house and left me standing between him and Jona. Was that the way it was going to be from now on?

"Glad you're feeling better," Jona said.

"Who says I am?"

Linc put his hand on my shoulder. "You all right?"

"Don't keep asking if I'm all right. I hate it when you do that."

Linc looked hurt. "I'm worried about you, that's all. You're not acting like yourself."

"What the hell does that mean, acting like myself? I just woke up, if you need an explanation for why I'm looking like I live on the street."

"You look good to me." Linc leaned over to kiss me. "Really good. In fact, you look the best."

Before Jona came along, I would have believed him. Linc was the kind of guy who was full of compliments and reassurances. Now I wasn't so sure.

"I'm sorry." I let him kiss me lightly on the lips. "You're right. I've been a little messed up lately." Linc put his arm around me and pulled me close.

Jona coughed to get our attention. "Can I use your washroom?"

"It's around the corner." I pointed down the hall.

Linc and I went into the kitchen.

"Why are you mad at me?" he asked when we were alone. "I don't know what I've done."

"Nothing." I didn't have time to say anything else, not with Jona set to come out of the bathroom at any moment. "We need to talk, though. Just you and me. But not now."

"For sure."

"I mean, without Jona."

"Yeah, I get it," he said.

Linc pressed me to his chest, and I could feel the movement of his breath in my hair. Standing close to him, I inhaled his scent: woodsmoke, sweat, and something more subtle—ferns, moss, the stream itself—just like it used to be.

When Jona walked around the corner, wiping his hands on his jeans, Linc stepped away from me. "Hey, man, what do you say we go home and change out of our wet clothes and then come back?"

I got the sense, from the way he said "we," that Jona would be returning with him, and that meant we wouldn't be having our private talk any time soon.

"That will give you time to wake up, Vik," Linc continued.

"Good idea," Jona replied. "These wet boxers are not fun."

"I know what you mean," Linc said. They laughed as if there was something I was missing.

Jona put his hand on Linc's shoulder and let it slide down his arm as he walked past him. As his fingers passed my eye level, I saw him clench lightly, as if he were giving Linc a private signal. Linc leaned toward Jona and tapped him on the back. I turned the other way when Linc bent to kiss me.

In a year, Linc and I had not had one serious disagreement. Now, since Jona had been in our lives, I felt like arguing with him every day.

As they walked down the front stairs, Linc and Jona were close enough that their arms brushed together. They climbed into the van and my stomach tied itself in a knot.

Suddenly I was desperate to get out of the house. I needed to run.

I stuffed my hand in my jacket pocket and pulled out a ten-dollar bill. After the van backed out of the driveway, I shut the front door behind me and ran down the stairs and up the road to TJ's market. I glanced at my watch. Even though it was usually only a four-minute run, it would be better than nothing.

I stopped when I turned into the parking lot and checked the time, three fifty-five. Almost my best time ever.

"Hey, Vik," TJ called out from behind the counter when I opened the door. "Long time no see."

Even though I went into the store at least once a day, TJ always said the same thing. He used to work with Bert at the mill. But he had seen the writing on the wall early, so by the time the mill shut down and everybody else got thrown out of work, TJ had already bought the store and was all set up. His market was like the town centre, and there wasn't much about anybody or anything that TJ didn't know.

"Hey, TJ."

I roamed the aisles, looking for something to eat. Finally I grabbed a few cartons of KD. Not exactly gourmet, but a sale sign said three for the price of two. So I picked up another box and headed to the till.

"Why don't you have one of these as well?" TJ said as he scanned the cartons. He handed me an apple from a basket on the counter.

"Sure, thanks." I rubbed it on my jeans. The waxy smudge it left made me think about eating crayons when I was a kid.

He passed me my change. "You all right, Vik?"

I wanted to say, *No, I'm not all right.* I had the feeling that TJ would understand. A few months earlier, when I was in the store, Bert had started yelling at me to hurry up. "Move it, Vik. You're getting as lazy as your lazy-ass Indian friends."

TJ was on him right away. "Not in my store," he told Bert in a voice loud enough for everyone in the building to hear. "Don't let me hear that bullshit talk around here."

I remember thinking, *This is where TJ gets punched.* But TJ stood right up to Bert, toe to toe. Bert didn't seem like such a tough guy then. He looked more like a pitiful old man.

When I saw TJ a few days later, he told me, "I went to school with your dad. He was a bully even back then."

"He's not my dad," I said. "He's Bert."

TJ nodded. "I hear ya."

Now I thought about saying, *My life sucks and I'm freaking out that I'm losing my boyfriend to a guy.* But I was too exhausted to get into it. The nightmare I'd had was messing with my head. So I faked a smile and said, "I'm fine."

"Take care of yourself, girl. And say hello to that nice young fellow you've got."

"Sure."

Back in the parking lot, I took a bite of the apple. It was red and glossy, but my teeth could barely penetrate the skin. The flesh was like rubbery chicken. I waited until I was out of TJ's sight before I spit the mouthful on the side of the road. I chucked the apple into the ditch.

Jona

"Are you sure I should be going back to Vik's with you?" I asked Linc as he drove me home. "You could ditch me, and that would give you a chance to talk to her alone."

"Yep, I'm sure," he said, without any hesitation. "It's all good."

All good? What was he thinking? I couldn't get out of Vik's fast enough. It wasn't just that Vik was unfriendly. The house itself made me nervous. Either Linc missed the whole thing or I was making it up, but Vik didn't look "all good" to me. Linc was a positive guy, but at some point you have to be blind to stay *that* positive.

"Didn't I hear Vik say she wanted to talk to you?"

"Yeah, but don't sweat it. We'll have time tonight."

Don't sweat it?

"Well, as long as it's okay for me to be at her place, and her dad doesn't come home. The last thing I want to do is see that guy again."

A few weeks earlier, Linc and I had run into Bert while we were getting gas. He stood by his car, at the next pump over from Linc's van, and said, "I don't know who you are, pretty boy, but I never want to see you anywhere near my place." Each word came out slowly and deliberately. "It's bad enough that Vik," he continued, "is dating this reserve clown. We don't need your type around here." I was so freaking terrified I almost peed myself. I wondered what he meant by "my type." I thought maybe he was referring to my purple running shoes or maybe my ponytail, but I didn't want to ask.

"Bert won't be home until midnight. But I'm thinking we should just go pick up Vik and bring her over to my place for the party tonight. She needs to get out of there. Believe me, I don't want to run into Bert myself."

Linc seemed to want, maybe even need, me to go back with him, and that made it a different story.

"Fifteen minutes?" He pulled up in front of the trailer.

"Yeah, okay," I said. "I'll risk it. But only for you."

I barely had time to change my clothes and find a couple of elastics before he was back. "That was only thirteen minutes."

He laughed. "The two-minute shower is my specialty."

"Are you kidding? You had time to shower?"

I knew the answer. His hair was gelled back, and he smelled amazing.

"Thanks for coming," he said as we drove up the road. "The truth is, this stuff with Vik is confusing the hell out of me."

He pushed the power button on the radio. "*Don't sit down, just don't sit down*" blasted out of the speaker, and I was thinking, "'*cause, babe, I'm coming to town.*" I smiled at my dumb-ass lyric attempt and sat back. Being needed was sexy. Damn sexy. I took a look at Linc and for the first time saw his vulnerable side. I might have been sixteen years old and batting zero in the relationship department, but I was coming alive.

Before we had moved to Carterton, I'd read a study that said guys think about sex anywhere from every seven seconds to every half hour. I was sure the study must be a fraud. How would anyone have time to think about anything else? It also worried me, though. On average, I thought about sex once a day, at the most. And they weren't pleasant thoughts. For instance, I was insanely terrified that if I ever did want to have sex, I wouldn't know how. Basically, I had diagnosed myself as off the chart for "failure to develop sexual tendencies."

That was before I met Linc. Now there was no way I could count how many times I'd thought about sex, even that morning alone. It was like my mind had a new screen saver. Every ten seconds or so, the image of Linc in his boxers flashed through my mind. Seeing his vulnerable side made it even worse. When I turned my head and saw him mouthing the words to the song on the radio—*God, the way he moves his lips!*—I had to think about jumping in the stream just to cool myself down.

Vik

I dumped the KD into boiling water. Then, as if someone had put a bullet in my gut, I threw my arms around my stomach and buckled over. I looked at my bare finger. It had been there. I could still feel the weight of the ring and the hard shapes of the stones on my palm. But now it was gone.

Could I have put it back and forgotten? Or was the whole thing a dream?

I raced to Dell and Bert's room. The door was open a crack, and the jewellery box sat in the middle of the dresser, exactly where I had left it. I did a mental review of every move I'd made since the last time I saw the ring: the bad dream, the clanging phone, Linc showing up unannounced, his hug, my run to TJ's, throwing the apple away. Why didn't I notice earlier that the ring was missing?

I picked up the piece of green velvet and shook it gently, as if by some magic the ring might appear. I did the same with the newspaper clipping and the satin ribbon. I was still in Dell and Bert's bedroom when I heard a knock. I raced out, slammed the bedroom door, and sucked in a couple of short breaths before bolting down the hall.

Linc opened the front door before I got there and called, "Honey, I'm home."

"Wow, that was quick," I stammered, my head in a scramble.

I pretended to shake my hands dry in a lame attempt to look like I'd been doing something legitimate.

"My trademark two-minute shower." He flexed like a bodybuilder. "That's all I needed, and now I'm yours."

He gripped me around the waist and did a waltzing dip. He was doing all the things that would, on a good day, make me laugh. But it was all I could do not to burst out crying. Especially when I noticed Jona standing right there behind him.

Jona

When Linc and I walked in, Vik was standing in the hall, looking like she was playing frozen tag. Her face was ghostly. Even when Linc grabbed her and started fooling around, she acted like a zombie.

What was going on with her? She looked terrified, as if the end of the world was coming.

When we got to the kitchen, she handed me a spoon and a bowl of KD. Although I hated the stuff, it solved two of my problems. I was ravenous, and eating gave me something to do.

I watched Vik and Linc standing side by side. By this time, Linc looked like he was watching the same damn disaster show as Vik. All I could think was how crazy and free I'd felt up the mountain. I was still itching to talk about what we'd done up there. Jesus, this was a downer. There was heavy shit going on, and I could feel it hanging in the room like a dead cat. Linc was right. Vik needed to get out of that house, and so did I.

I was wishing for Ashley's canned chili and thinking how great it would have tasted up at the stream. By this time I had almost finished the KD, and it was sitting in my gut as if I'd dropped a medicine ball down there. I broke the silence in the room.

"Can I use the bathroom?" I asked Vik and then laughed. "Again."

"Yeah." She ignored my attempt at humour and gave a vague wave toward the kitchen door.

I sat on the can long enough to let my gut cramps ease off. Then I decided I should stay in there for a few extra minutes to give Vik and Linc time to clear up whatever the hell was going on between them.

From what I could see, relationships were like chaos theory: a million variables all messing with each other, with millions and millions of possible outcomes. It didn't matter how much humans wanted things to be logical. The truth was, we could never know which one of those million possibilities was going to make the next thing happen.

It was like the butterfly effect—when the wings of a butterfly disrupt the air in Mexico, they can trigger a hurricane in Louisiana, which might cause a tornado in China. How can you know? It was like trying to figure out what the hell was going on with Vik. Maybe a climber in Tibet had fallen off a mountain, and that had made a lion eat a tourist in Mozambique, which was causing Vik to be caught up in some sort of tragedy here in Carterton. Who knew?

And though chaos theory was a pretty cool way to describe the problem, it sure as hell didn't come up with the solutions. In any case, it was Linc and Vik's problem, so I decided to just leave it to them and walk home. I would catch up with them at the party. I was feeling too good to get all serious.

As I left the bathroom, I heard voices outside the front door, then the handle turning. I walked down the hall toward the kitchen, glancing back at the front door. Freaking hell! Bert was coming into the house. I turned and sprinted into the kitchen to warn Vik and Linc, but for one brief moment my eyes met Bert's.

Vik and Linc swung around, panic pulling their faces tight as they heard Bert's voice. Vik let go of Linc and dropped into a chair next to me. He stepped back a couple of paces, as if he had been hit by a gust of wind.

I felt time slow down, as if each split second would be our last, and there was a humming in my ears, so loud I could barely hear Bert's words. He must have been talking to Vik's mom at first, but now he was yelling with rage. I eyed the back door. Instinct told me to run like hell, but I couldn't move. Vik looked over at Linc, her eyes saying *save me*, and it threw him into damage control. He took a step toward the door, ready to meet Bert head-on.

By the time Bert barged into the kitchen, his face was bright red and his body was shaking furiously.

"What the hell is that res van doing parked outside?" He sounded like he was speaking into a bullhorn. His eyes bored into me. "And what the hell is that little fuck-fag doing in my house?"

It was surreal. Scared as I was, I felt like I was a spectator at a performance, where everyone was playing a role. Linc's chest got bigger and bigger as if, like Alice in Wonderland, he could fill the whole room. Vik had folded herself up in a chair and become as small as a mouse. Her mom, like a bobble-head, kept appearing and disappearing in the kitchen doorway. Bert expanded like a giant bellows, like the evil lion brother in *The Lion King*. I thought he would pop and explode all over the room at any moment.

But with four of us in the little kitchen, it was no stage. We were close enough that the rank smell of Bert's sweat and the stale smoke on his clothes made me gag.

Linc stepped toward Bert. "We just came to pick up Vik and now we're leaving." His voice was much louder than usual, and I was thinking, *What a great act.*

Then, like a cat, Vik sprang out of her chair. She tugged my jacket sleeve and said, "Let's go."

I staggered forward, and Vik moved in behind me. Using me for a barricade, she pushed past Bert into the hall. His hand shot out to catch me, but Linc leaned between us and cleared the way so we could keep going.

Once we got into the hall, I started running, and Vik must have let go. I didn't stop until I was outside, down the stairs, and around the far side of the van. I opened the door.

"Get in, Vik," I said.

But when I looked behind me, she wasn't there.

Vik

When I heard the front door open, I thought Jona had gone outside to get something from Linc's van. But it was Bert's voice in the hall. "Fucking three hours on the road to get there and home. And you got the fucking day wrong. Goddammit, Dell. And what the hell is that res van doing parked outside?"

By the time Bert stormed into the kitchen, I had pulled myself together enough to know that we had to get out of there. I knew what Bert was capable of doing, so I pushed Jona into the hall ahead of me. Linc made space for us to get past, but Bert caught my arm and I lurched back and stumbled into him and Linc.

Linc gripped Bert's wrist. "Oh, no, you don't. Not while I'm around." He squeezed until Bert let go of me.

Bert was shorter and older and a bad match for Linc, but he didn't give in.

"I'm telling you, boy." He stood glaring at Linc, with his eyes narrowed to a slit. "It's bad enough to come home and find you in my house uninvited, let alone your poofy-ass boyfriend. Vik, is this the best you can do? Indians and purple-shoed faggots?"

"Come on, Linc," I said. "Let's go."

Linc had Bert pinned to the wall, but that didn't mean he shut up. "Where the hell do you think you're going?" he shouted. His arms flailed around, trying to get a piece of me.

"None of your business. Just out," I screamed.

Droplets of Bert's spit sprayed across the hall. "You're not going any damn where."

When Linc let him go, Bert jerked his elbow back. His eyes were like hollow sockets. I closed my own eyes, expecting to feel Bert's fist slam into me. But I heard a body hit the wall and looked up in time to see Bert slip down into a heap on the floor.

Linc bent over him. "Not while I'm here, Bert," he repeated. "And I don't care whose house this is."

"Fuck you, Victoria! Your fucking Indian boyfriend just assaulted me in my own home! Dell, don't just stand there like a useless twat! Call the fucking cops!"

"Let's go!" Linc grabbed my hand and we ran out the door to the van and leaped in. Linc started the engine.

"Holy shit," he said. "Where's Jona?"

There wasn't time to look for him, so he took off. A few minutes later we found him on the road, hurrying toward home.

Linc stopped, and Jona got in the back seat. I turned to the window. Burning tears poured down my cheeks.

Jona leaned forward and asked me, "You okay?"

How should I answer that? What could I possibly say? My family freak show had been on display like a circus act, with Linc and Jona in front-row seats.

Curl up and die. The phrase was invented for times like this. Linc passed me a hand towel from his door pocket. I buried my face in it and took a deep breath. The smell of Linc's sweat calmed me a bit. But nothing was okay. I had no idea how I would ever get out of the mess I was in. I should have told Linc about the ring as soon as he arrived, but how could I possibly do that now? What had happened was humiliating enough.

Linc's eyes met Jona's in the rearview mirror. "Sorry about that, man. I never expected Vik's old man to show up."

"No worries. I'll get over it."

"Yeah, but what an asshole. I've seen him mouth off before, but this time he went bloody ballistic. I felt like taking him out when I heard him call you that shit."

I'd said the same things about Bert myself. But I had never heard Linc talk about my family like that. Not when he heard Bert screaming at me on the phone one Sunday when I wasn't home to cut the lawn. Not even the time Bert found us in my room, or later, when I showed Linc the bruises on my face.

What about me? Why is Linc more offended by what Bert said to Jona than the brutal shit he's done to me?

When Linc put his hand on my leg, I pushed it away.

Bert and Dell were my biology, which made me feel like an alien, and there was nothing I could do about it. But now I felt like an alien even with Linc. Maybe especially with Linc.

Stop it, Vik, I said to myself. *Linc isn't your biggest problem. Jona isn't even your biggest problem. Not now. You've lost the damn ring.*

Remembering that sent chills up my spine. If Bert had been out of his mind earlier, wait until he found out the ring was missing. I tried to convince myself that it wasn't *really* lost. It had to be in one of three places: the long grass between the cave and the house, the cave itself, or, the worst possible scenario, somewhere in the hedgerow. Or maybe on the road between our house and TJ's. Or even in the kitchen. But, in any case, the ring could be found. My problem was timing. I had left the box out, so as soon as Bert or Dell went into their bedroom, they would discover the ring was missing. I could not return the ring to the jewellery box without them knowing I had taken it out.

I had to tell Linc. If only I could get him alone, I'd tell him everything, and he would help me figure out what to do.

When we stopped in Linc's driveway, he leaned over and kissed my cheek. "I need to run—gotta pee. I'll see you in a few minutes. Okay?"

Before Linc was gone, Ruby appeared on the van's passenger side, and it was then I remembered the party. Everybody from SOS was gathering to celebrate, and we'd invited other kids from the reserve, too. How would I manage to talk to Linc alone?

"Vik!" Ruby threw the van door open. "I'm so happy you're feeling better, girl. Wait till you see what we did at the stream today! Thanks to Jona, who found the seedlings. They're all planted—finished. One stream down, and on to the next." She held up her hand for a high-five. "Whoo hooo!!"

I gave her a limp response as we walked toward the house. "Good for you guys."

She put her arm around me. "God, poor you. You still look like death."

Billy was leaning against Ashley, who had her butt hitched up on the porch rail. He raised his beer when Jona got out of the van. "Party time!"

"We missed you so much today, Vik," Ashley said. "Leon got the instructions from Ian. But Jona was the star. Without him, we wouldn't have had any damn seedlings to plant."

All right already. Wasn't it enough that the newest member of our committee turned out to be the smartest guy in the world? Did everyone have to keep singing his praises? Even Ruby seemed to be madly in love with the guy.

I tuned out their voices. *What does it matter? Jona's not your worst problem right now,* I reminded myself.

A hockey game blared from the TV in the living room. Leon and a bunch of kids I didn't know well were eating chips and cookies. No one looked up when I walked through to the kitchen.

When Sandy saw me, she put her arms around me and gave me a tight hug. "Sit down, honey," she said. She put her hands on my shoulders and lowered me onto a chair. "How are you?"

Tell Sandy, I thought. *She'll help you straighten things out if anyone can.*

If I'd been able to choose a mom from all the moms I'd ever met, I'd have picked Sandy. She was the sort of mom you'd want to have holding your hand when you got a root canal at the dentist.

"Today has been the worst day of my life," I told her.

Linc must have filled her in briefly on what had happened because she said, "It must be hard. Your dad has never been an easy guy."

I took a deep breath. "It's not only that. This morning I—"

Before I had time to say any more, Ruby ran into the kitchen, interrupting us. "Come on, Vik. Come on, Auntie. You don't want to miss this. Jona's going to improv a song about working up at the stream."

Sandy put her arms around my shoulders. "We can talk later, honey. Let's hear the song first. It'll do you good."

Ruby pulled on my sleeve, and I had no choice but to follow her to the living room. Sandy and I stood on either side of the kitchen doorway.

Jona was sitting on the sofa with his guitar on his knee. "I didn't say I had a song about today, Ruby," he protested.

"No, you said you'd make one up."

Jona had no idea how persistent Ruby could be.

"How about later tonight?" he begged. "How about tomorrow?"

Linc stood up and mimed holding a microphone. "And now, Jona Prince," he said in a deep voice, then turned to Jona. "Give us what you've got."

How could everybody be having so much fun when my world was falling apart?

"Okay, maybe I'll start with something I've been working on," Jona said.

He started strumming his guitar, and Ruby got the remote and muted the TV. The last thing I wanted to do was listen to Jona sing, but I couldn't think of a way to leave.

When the house phone rang, Sandy went back into the kitchen to answer it. She handed me the receiver.

I stared at it, sitting in the palm of my hand, and thought about hanging up. It would only delay the inevitable, but at least I'd have time to tell Sandy everything. But Sandy had walked across the living room and was sitting on a pillow on the floor next to Linc. He and the others all had their attention glued on Jona.

What choice did I have? I walked back through the kitchen and sat down on the stairs in the hall.

"Yeah?"

Dell shrieked into the phone, "It must have been Jona. That damn weirdo. I knew we couldn't trust him."

Why wasn't she calling my cell, and how had she gotten Linc's home number? I couldn't think about that; I was too confused by what she was saying.

Bert shouted in the background, "I'll kill that fucking kid. Tell him, Dell. Tell him I'll kill him."

"Shut up, Bert." Dell was hysterical. "You won't kill anyone."

Bert started to cough. "And you know I'll do it."

This was making no sense. Bert was furious that Linc and Jona had come over, that I'd run out of the house, that Linc had pushed him. I could understand that. But why were they talking about killing Jona?

I could hear Bert wheezing as he wrestled the phone away from Dell. "It's that fucking homo friend you've been hanging around with lately," he screamed. I held the phone away from my ear. "We've got the police coming, and that scumbag is going to pay for this."

"What the hell are you talking about?"

"Dell's ring," he hollered. "That stupid asshole of a kid stole Dell's ring. What the fuck were you thinking, inviting him into this house?"

I swallowed hard to keep from upchucking the few mouthfuls of KD I had forced down earlier. I looked at the phone, trying to make sense of what I was hearing. The ring hadn't been stolen. It was lost. And I was the one who had done it. What the hell did Jona have to do with it?

I put my hand over the receiver so Bert couldn't hear Jona singing in the other room.

"That ring means everything to us. Without it we're nothing. That kid was looking for something to steal, and he went into the bedroom. He's so damn dumb that he left her jewellery box wide open with all the evidence plain as day in pure daylight."

My body went cold. I opened my mouth to say, "Jona didn't steal the ring. I lost it. It's outside somewhere in the backyard. I can find it." But my throat clenched tight, and no words came out.

“I’ll kill whoever took that ring,” he hollered. “I don’t give a shit who it is.”

Me, I thought. *You would kill me, wouldn’t you?* My hands were shaking as I held the phone.

There was a crash at the other end of the line, then the sound of dishes splintering on the floor. Dell screeched, “You’re a freaking psychopath. You hit me.” She broke into a wail I’d heard too many times before. Her voice was like a tinny bell ringing from the bottom of a deep pit.

“Vik?” Bert lowered his voice. “Are you there, girl? Now listen to your poor mother. She’s lost everything.”

Dell’s crying got louder, then faded again, as if Bert had held the phone up close to her to prove his point.

“I’ve called the cops. We’ve told them everything.” Bert’s voice was even quieter now. “But I’m going to get that boy before they have a chance to protect the little scum. Is he there with you?”

“No.” My heart sped up.

“Where is he, Vik? Does he live on that fucking reserve?”

“No. I don’t know where he lives.”

Dell was still whimpering. “There, there,” he said softly. “I’ll take care of this, Delly.” The sugary sweet voice he always used after beating on Dell terrified me. Thankfully he never bothered with that bullshit when he was messing with me.

“No, Berty, don’t do it.” Dell’s voice was meek, like a little girl’s. “Let the cops take care of it.”

“The damn cops won’t do a thing to a kid. By the time they get here, he’ll be on his way to town to sell your ring. Dell, we’ll be ruined. You still there, Victoria?”

“What?” I could barely squeeze a whisper out. Much as I

wished I could tell him to fuck off when he got loud and belligerent, I couldn't do a thing. "What am I supposed to do?"

"You don't have to do a damn thing. I'll find him and take care of the little bastard."

There was a clunk, and then a door slammed. I jumped a mile.

"Bert?" I had an image of Bert snatching his rifle out of the cupboard and cruising around in search of Jona. "Bert? Bert?" I muttered.

Dell came back on the line. "Vik, I can't stop him. The cops will take their own sweet time getting here. What's the kid going to do with the ring before that?"

Can't stop him? Or won't? They were like Bonnie and Clyde—partners in crime.

But she was right about the cops being slow. There was no police station in Carterton. If we were lucky, a cop from Simpson Mills might show up forty-five minutes after getting a call. If a miracle happened, and the cops were already in the area, they might show up quicker. Or they might not.

"Do something to stop him, Dell," I pleaded.

"You know I can't." She started to sob.

We stayed on the line for a minute or so without saying anything. I tried to gather up the courage to tell her. *It was me. I took the ring outside and lost it.*

Ruby stuck her head around the corner. "You missed the greatest song ever."

I pointed to the phone. She threw her hands up. "Hurry and finish. He's going to sing another one."

I stared at the phone in my hand. What could I say? It was one thing to tell Dell the truth once I had the ring in my hand.

It was another thing to do it now, before I knew for sure the ring could be found. For all I knew, Bert was going to burst in to Linc's place at any moment, his rifle cocked, ready to shoot Jona. If he knew I had anything to do with the ring's disappearance, he would be coming after me.

"Well, then, what the hell do you expect me to do?" I said.

"I don't know," she said.

"I have to go, Dell," I said. "I'll let you know if I think of something."

I pressed *Off* and went into the bathroom. My gut was going to explode. I didn't know whether to stick my head in the toilet or get my butt on the seat.

Jona

Unwind, the bind,
find yourself in the pretty bow, bro,
blow the angel wings off the dandelion.

Holy shit, what a day. From the freaking high on the hill to running for my life from Vik's dad, and now, less than an hour later, I was singing for a bunch of kids I hardly knew. It was not exactly what I had expected from this little bush town.

I stopped for a break after my first song. "I need water," I said, putting my guitar down.

"Can I see?" Ashley pointed to my guitar. She looked like she was in downtown Vancouver on a Saturday night, wearing a silky lavender T with a gold lamé vest and jean miniskirt that showed off her long legs right down to her white sneakers.

"Sure." I handed it over.

She put one foot on a stool so she could cradle it on her thigh, then strummed, badly.

"Ouch," she said. "How long you been playing?"

"Seven or eight years now."

She picked out a few notes. "Ow. That does not sound good. It's not easy. You take lessons?"

"Sort of. I learned from an old guy who let me hang around his place with a bunch of musicians."

"Your people sing?" By now I knew that when First Nations

kids used the term "your people," they meant the tribe I was from, not the city or neighbourhood.

"I don't know." I didn't want to admit that my dad had been a musician, because then she'd start asking a whole lot of questions I didn't want to answer.

"Would you teach me?"

"Sure, if you want." She passed me the guitar back. Ruby had brought me a drink, so I took a gulp and started to strum. "It's one of my dreams," I said. "To be a musician."

"You look like one already."

"I'll take that as a compliment."

She smiled. "No other guy around here would wear a ponytail."

"I hope I can take that as a compliment as well."

"You bet."

Billy burst into the room. "Bro," he said. Something must have happened on the mountain, because Billy had gotten over his edge with me. "Let's have some more tunes."

"We still need that song for the stream," Ruby said. "How about that improv you promised us?"

I tried to ignore her as I concentrated on tuning. The idea of improvising something while people listened scared the shit out of me. Then, *wham*, I got a hit of déjà vu. I was a little kid watching my dad sitting on a brown leather sofa in someone's living room. His bum was hooked on the edge of the cushion to make room for his guitar on his lap. He was jamming. His sound was exquisite. His lyrics were something about a mask, but they didn't stick in my head.

God, I thought, *it could have been George's place, with a bunch of people with guitars, drums, triangles, and rattles.*

I hunched forward and took the stance I pictured my dad in, then started strumming again, hoping something brilliant would come to mind. People were calling for me to get going.

"I can't call it up like an order of fries, you know," I told them. "I can't make a song right before your eyes." I tried to string some words together.

I closed my eyes and saw Dad's guitar. It was blond maple or birch with mother-of-pearl marquetry. An eagle design swooped across the top, under the strings and over the side, making a 3-D effect.

I started a *ta, ta, ta, tata, ta* drumbeat on the body of my guitar, then finger-picked a few notes. A rhythm started to flow, riffing off a couple of sequences I'd thought of a few weeks earlier. Then I had one of those magical moments that musicians and poets pray for. My brain stopped trying and let the words, the guitar, the tune, and my voice work it out together. I started to sing.

I'm an addict with no beer, a Christmas carol with no cheer
a mask without a face, a silent prayer with no grace
I'm a car without its wheels, a dealer with no deals
A woman with no breasts, a sleeper who doesn't rest

I'm a promise that is hollow, intention with no follow through
babe, I wanna be somebody
I just wanna be somebody

I wanna be your morning star, I wanna drive a classic car
I wanna be, wanna wanna be
Somebody

People were clapping, and some of the girls sang along. The

beat quickened, and I felt more words coming. While I waited, I beat my guitar again and chanted. "*Hey, hey hey, ho, ho, heyaaa, heyaaa.*" The room followed my lead.

I'm a boy with no guts, an artist in a rut
I'm a tree planter with no trees, a swimmer in the breeze
a skinny boy with bony knees

I'm the one who reads the books
Until I got a real look...a real look, a real look
Until I got a real look and had an epiphany
Cause I'm a visionary
A missionary, an emissary, a revolutionary with an epiphany
I wanna be somebody
Wanna make a crazy scene, wanna fill your every dream
Wanna change the world

The SOS is going to change these hills
The SOS is going to change these hills
hey, hey, heyoooo

As the song faded, I flashed back to that scene of Dad sitting on the leather sofa. He was smiling. His eyes were like black glass, and I saw my reflection in them. Was I really at home? In Carterton? Were these my people?

I started tapping my purple-leather-high-top-shoed foot. Did I find the real Jona Prince up on the hill?

Vik

In Linc's bathroom, I sat on the toilet and leaned over the sink at the same time. After a few minutes the nausea passed, along with everything in my body that could be flushed away or washed down the sink.

I stood up shakily. Why did people put mirrors in front of the toilet? My face had no colour, as if my blood had been drained by a vampire.

I splashed cold water on my cheeks. When I opened the door, I found Sandy waiting for me in the hall.

"You sick?" she asked.

"Better now. But I still don't feel very well."

She sat down beside me on the stairs.

"Did something happen on the phone?"

"Yeah."

Sandy pulled me against her. It was awkward at first. She was only a little taller than me, but her breasts and stomach made her perfectly round, and she felt like a soft pillow. Her shape showed her age. Otherwise, she didn't look old enough to be Linc's mom.

"Breathe, honey." She rubbed my shoulder with one hand. "Take your time. I'm not going anywhere."

But she didn't know that every second counted. Bert was probably on his way here, looking for Jona, and he might be carrying a gun. If he found Jona, he might use it. He would use it on me, too, if he knew the truth about what I did.

"I...I...I," I sputtered. Could I really tell Sandy? Tell her that I had taken our family's inheritance outside, into my childhood sanctuary, so that I could daydream about being someone else, someone rich and important, and then lost it? How pathetic was that?

Sandy thought I was strong. She had nominated me for the "Youth of the Year" award for the work I did setting up SOS. She thought I was a teen on a mission to make the world a better place. She didn't know that my life was a complete disaster. But I couldn't worry about that now. I had to tell her the truth.

I had read on the Internet that if you held your breath you deprived your brain of oxygen, and that made you stupid. So I sucked in a big breath, then another, and swallowed it like a gulp of water. Stupid sure wasn't what I needed right now.

Sandy stroked my arm. She had beautiful fingers, with perfectly oval nails painted in zebra stripes. Their softness soothed me.

"Linc brought Jona over to my place this afternoon," I started.

"I heard. I'll talk to Jona. He doesn't deserve that man's abuse. God knows what it must be like for you to live with him."

"Sandy, it's not about Bert being an ass to Jona. He may be on his way over here right now. Maybe even with a gun."

She swung around so she was squatting on the floor in front of me, looking at me eye to eye. "What do you mean?"

"That was Bert on the phone. He thinks Jona stole something from our house and he's threatening to kill him."

"Holy crap."

"We have to do something. Bert can be really dangerous."

"I know. You don't need to convince me about Bert."

I doubted that she *really* knew what I meant, but I wanted to ask her what *she* meant. What did she know about Bert? First I had to tell her the part about me losing the ring in the backyard.

She held on to my hands for a second or two, then jumped up. "I'm going to make a phone call. I'll be right back."

Before she had time to get to the phone, there was a loud knock on the door. Sandy glanced back at me, fear in her eyes. Then, as if time slowed down to register each one of her movements, she walked through the kitchen and the living room toward the front door.

I stared at the door, unable to breathe. I imagined it bursting open and Bert starting to fire randomly around the room. Blood would spatter the walls, and kids would scream as their bodies flew through the air and flopped one on top of the other. I'd be left standing. I'd be the only one still alive with the man people called my father. I'd look into his bloodthirsty face, and then he'd pump two, three, or maybe all the rest of his bullets into me. I wondered if he would leave me on the driveway or throw me in the back of the car. Would he drop me somewhere on the way home?

I leaned forward on the stairs. Linc appeared in the living room, coming from the other direction, and I watched him and Sandy reach for the door handle at the same time.

I jumped up and ran through the kitchen, opening my mouth to scream *Don't open it* just as Linc pulled the door toward him.

Light poured in around the forms of two cops. One was tall and broad like a bulldog. The other was thin and only came up to the big cop's shoulders.

The room went silent. Sandy stepped in front of Linc to greet the men.

The big cop said, "I'm Sergeant Hopper, and this is Constable Mainwaring. Is Jona Prince here?"

Sandy's voice was strong and steady. "This is my house, officer." Both cops rocked back on their heels. "I'd like to know why you are here."

"We're looking for Jona Prince. Are you his mother?"

"No, I'm not. What do you want him for?"

"We are here in regard to the theft of a ring that took place this afternoon in Carterton. Luckily, we were out this way. We need to find this boy and take him in for questioning."

I stepped sideways and cowered in the kitchen, stunned. How could this be happening?

"Jona was up the mountain today with these other kids, planting trees," Sandy said. "How could he have stolen a ring? You're not making any sense."

"We need to talk to him," the big cop repeated. "Is there someone by that name here?"

Everyone started talking at once.

"Chill out, Officer."

"We're just listening to a little music."

"Jona's done what?"

"We're not causing any trouble."

"What the fuck are you talking about? Jona's no thief."

Then I heard Billy say, "Yeah. I'm Jona and he's Jona and that guy over there, he's Jona too." The room busted up with laughter.

After a few moments, Sandy's voice drowned the rest out. "Yes, Jona's here, but I'm sure this is a big mistake. Jona didn't steal anything."

The room went totally silent. I peeked around the corner. The cops were looking from one boy to the next, trying to figure out which one was the real Jona.

"We are here to take Jona Prince in for questioning, ma'am," the big cop said. "We'll have an investigation before we'll know whether or not he stole anything."

"So what you're telling me," Sandy said, "is that someone has accused Jona Prince of stealing?"

"We've got a witness, ma'am. Someone saw this Jona Prince in the act. I want to know which of these boys is him." His voice got a little louder, as if maybe the main problem was that the real Jona hadn't heard him. "I want him to stand up and come with us down to the station for questioning."

"Who the hell are you guys, anyways, coming around here like this?" Billy jumped to his feet.

Linc shoved Billy back onto the chair. "Leave it alone, cousin."

This is your chance, Vik, I told myself. *Be courageous. Stand up. Tell them the truth.* That seemed crazy, though. My story would sound so weird, I doubted the cops would even believe me. And how could I get up in front of everyone and explain what had happened? This was becoming more of a nightmare by the second.

"Do you know that a madman just phoned here looking for Jona Prince as well?" Sandy demanded. "Do you know that he threatened to kill Jona Prince? Maybe Jona is not your problem."

Billy was on his feet again. "Yeah, asshole. Maybe you should be looking elsewhere."

Linc held his arm up to hold Billy back. "What the hell are you talking about?" he said to the cops. "This is insane."

Jona stared at the cops, looking as confused as I felt. His face was pale, and he was clenching his guitar as if it were a shield.

The short cop said to Sandy, "We'll look into that, ma'am. I'll make sure I report what you've said to the station."

"I'm not going to tell you which one is Jona Prince," she said. "If he wants to go in with you, I'll leave that up to him."

There was a long pause. I jammed my eyes shut and opened them just in time to see Jona walk toward the police.

"I'm Jona." His voice was barely loud enough to hear. His head was down, and when he reached the big cop he put his hands forward, as if his moves had been choreographed in Hollywood.

All of a sudden, Billy charged up behind him. "Don't go with them, bro."

I don't know what Billy thought he was doing. Maybe he intended to pull Jona away. But that was not what happened. All I could see was Jona's body hit the big cop. When the cop pushed him away, Jona grabbed the cop's arm, trying to keep his balance, and a split second later the cop had him on the floor. Billy slunk back to his seat as if he wasn't the one who had started the whole thing. It would have been a comedy in a different place and time.

The big cop lifted Jona off the ground with one hand and—*clink, clink, clink*—cuffed him.

I stayed back as everyone followed Jona out the door like a funeral procession. They stood in a huddle on the front porch as the tall cop ushered him down the stairs. I stood at the window and watched him slam the car door.

Sandy followed the short cop and was telling him something. I couldn't make out what she was saying, but I figured she was filling him in on the threats Bert had made on the phone.

The cop nodded and climbed into the front passenger seat. As the cop car drove away, I caught a glimpse of Jona, looking no bigger than a kid, in the back seat.

I was ashamed of my feelings, but there was something reassuring about seeing Jona leave. He was safe, at least. Bert couldn't get him now. I might have wanted him out of my life and Linc's, but he didn't deserve this. He didn't deserve what Bert could do to him, either. But having him at the cop shop gave me time. Maybe I could sneak back home and somehow find the ring. I would tell the cops the real story, and then this nightmare would be over.

It sounded easy, but how the hell was I going to do it? I felt like running out the back door and not stopping until I reached the city. I'd go to Victoria or Vancouver and find a new life. But what about Jona? And what about Bert? What if I ran into him?

There was no running away. Somehow I had to find the guts to face this.

Jona

The big cop, Hopper, stopped when we got to the police car. "We're bringing you in for questioning, kid, regarding the theft of a ring from the Fromski house." He opened the back door of the police car. Holding my arm with one hand, he shielded my head with the other and gave me a solid shove into the back seat.

"And don't bother messing with us." He held the door open while I shuffled my butt along the seat. Then he leaned in close enough that I could smell his foul breath. "It's not like there are any other suspects. You and your buddy Linc were the only ones at the house this afternoon, and someone saw you at the scene, so don't waste our time trying to talk yourself out of this one."

When he slammed the door, I got hit with an even worse stench. I'd read somewhere that there are different kinds of sweat. It's an evolutionary thing. Stress sweat stinks worse than jogging or biking sweat. The disgusting smell is supposed to scare away the wild animals that are chasing you. I lifted my arm and took a whiff. I reeked, though it wasn't going to be enough to scare these guys off. I felt sick as I thought about everyone who had ever sat in the back seat of that car, sweating buckets of stress sweat and suffocating, like me, from the collective stench. Feeling like an idiot with my hands cuffed together, I pulled my sweatshirt up over my nose to mask the smell.

What the hell? He says I stole a ring from the Fromski house? Who's Fromski? It must be Vik's place, but isn't her last name Buckingham? But I wasn't anywhere else today. Except up the mountain. Was that what Sandy was talking about when she said a maniac had phoned? Vik's dad? What the hell?

I tried to put the pieces together, but nothing made sense. I replayed every move I made at Vik's house. *When did I have time to steal a ring? Where could it have been? What sort of ring would they have that would be worth stealing? This must be a mistake. Surely to God they'll sort it all out.*

The whole thing seemed like a movie. Maybe one of those old Hitchcock movies Mom watched on TV, where people were always getting nailed for stuff they didn't do. Or more like an Adam Sandler flick, where everyone plays an ass. Billy's performance was genius—a brilliant act of solidarity, telling the cops everyone there was named Jona. I could see it pissed the big cop off, and for a few moments I had to admire Billy's style. But then I figured things would get messy unless I fessed up to being the real Jona. Whatever that meant.

Vik

I flopped back down on the stairs at Linc's as reality started to hit me. Was Jona really going to be charged with stealing the ring? That was horrible enough in itself. But was I the only one who could put a stop to what was happening? What if I couldn't find the ring? What the hell was I supposed to do? I didn't accuse him.

I told myself to start by eating my pride and telling Sandy. *It's the right thing to do and it's not that hard. She'll understand,* I thought. Maybe if I told Linc, as well, the three of us could look for the ring in my backyard. I just needed to take Sandy aside. So why was I sitting on the stairs instead?

Back in the living room, I could hear everyone talking at once.

"Jona wouldn't steal anything."

"What bullshitter is accusing him?"

"Must be some white guy who doesn't like First Nations. They think we're sneaking around wanting their white shit."

"Damn white fuckers are always out to get us."

"Racist pigs!"

"I hate white people."

Their words were so nasty it shocked me. I could even hear Ashley and Ruby, but Billy's voice was the loudest. "Let's go get them. I'll whip their white butts."

I shuddered. I had always tried not to annoy Billy. He reminded me too much of Bert.

The one voice I didn't hear saying anything was Linc's. Thank God. But I didn't hear him telling them to shut up, either.

When I first met Linc, I'd felt out of place with his friends, an outsider. White girls weren't very welcome on the reserve. But it had been more than a year now, and I thought his friends and family had accepted me. I felt close to Ruby, especially. Now, though, I wondered how I had been naïve enough to believe that these were my friends too.

Come on, Linc, I said silently. *Please. I need you to defend me. Whites are my people. We aren't all bad.*

But Linc said nothing at all.

Finally Sandy yelled, "Stop it. All of you. You are in my house. You might think you have good reasons to hate white people, but hate talk is hate talk and it sucks. I don't put up with your bullshit any more than theirs."

Except for a few people mumbling things I couldn't hear, the room got quiet.

Then Linc finally spoke up. "She's right, you guys. That's brutal stuff. We don't even know what happened."

Was that all he could say? And only after his mother spoke up first?

I had to get out of there. I checked my cell for the bus schedule. If I left right away and hitchhiked, I could probably get to the bus stop in Simpson Mills by eight. I'd be in time for the eight-thirty bus to Victoria. *If I miss the bus,* I thought, *I'll run.* The way I was feeling, I figured I could run all the way. The hell with Bert; I would take the risk.

I was moving toward the back door when Sandy appeared beside me. "Vik, did you hear all that?"

I nodded. How could I have missed it?

She put her arm around me and guided me back to the stairs. By that time, Linc and Ruby were standing beside her.

"Everyone has gone ballistic," Sandy said. "They were upset about Jona, but that's no excuse."

Linc was having trouble meeting my eyes. "Jesus, I'm sorry you heard that shit, babe."

Sorry I heard it? How about sorry your friends genuinely hate me? How can I tell any one of them what happened after hearing the vicious things everyone was saying?

My shoulders started to heave.

Linc sat down behind me and rubbed my back. "They're just mad, Vik. And no one knows what's going on."

I stopped sobbing long enough to say, "Since when does mad mean you can say shit like that?" Then my sobs exploded.

"It's okay, Vik. I hear you," Linc said.

"It's not okay," I blubbered. "When Bert says that shit I go to bat for you."

"But no one knows what's going on."

"Exactly. Nobody knows what happened. But it's like, Jona's one of us, so he couldn't have done it."

Ruby passed me some tissue. "I don't get it. Are you saying Jona's guilty of something?"

"No. I didn't say that. I'm just feeling beat up right now. That shit was hard to hear." I wasn't even sure of Ruby anymore.

God, if only I could just disappear, now that I know what they really think of me.

What does it matter what they think of you? I thought. *Just tell them all. What do you care? Just freaking do something to stop the chaos.* I needed things to line up—I needed order back in my life.

I started talking without thinking about what I was going to say. "That was Bert on the phone. He said that after Linc and Jona and I ran out of the house this afternoon, they found Dell's jewellery box open and her expensive ring was gone. He said it was going to ruin our family."

Essentially, that was what Bert had said.

"What do you mean, ruin you?" Ruby asked.

"The ring was my grandma's—she had a ton of money, and she left the ring to my mom when she died."

"So why aren't *you* rich?"

"Ruby!" Sandy cut her off.

"Bert thinks one day he'll sell it and make a killing. But none of that matters, because on the phone, Bert said he thinks Jona's the one who took it. And he said that he'll kill him."

"There's no way Jona would do that," Linc said. "And you were there all day today, Vik. The ring can't be missing."

"It is. It's gone." That part of the story I was sure about. "But you're not listening. Bert could be here any minute. He might have his gun."

I took a deep breath, gathered all the courage I could muster, and continued. "I know Jona didn't take the ring—what Bert is saying is a lie."

The front door slammed. The four of us jumped, and Sandy bolted into the living room. When she returned, she had the phone in her hand. "Billy just came in from having a smoke," she said. "But I'm calling the cops. They need to stop Bert."

With the cops who'd taken Jona heading back to Simpson Mills, we weren't likely to see any other police for an hour, even if they sent someone right out.

I waited while she phoned. "Yes, that's right. Bert Fromski.

He threatened to kill a young man. Jona Prince. Yes, the boy who's being brought in right now. Yes, I know I told the constable, but we are afraid Bert is still dangerous."

She ended the call and tossed the phone on the table. "Shit. Those cops are useless."

Oh my God, I thought. *Where did my courage go? How do I get started again?* I needed everyone to sit still, calm down. I couldn't tell them while they were all running around.

Linc said, "Bert's a liar. Jona wouldn't steal Dell's ring. I know him."

Of course Bert was bullshitting. I'd just said it myself. From the front door he couldn't have seen Jona coming out of the bedroom, and he had no proof Jona stole the ring, because the ring wasn't stolen. So why did I hate it so much when Linc called Bert a liar?

"The ring is missing. It's all my family has. It's natural for Bert to freak about it." *Holy,* I thought, *me defending Bert to Linc? How messed up is that?*

Linc said, "I hear you. I'm just saying, I wouldn't put it past Bert to make shit up to nail Jona."

I wrapped my arms around myself and squeezed, trying to stop my body from vibrating, and wished I was at home. I needed to shut myself in my bedroom, curl up in my blankie, and knit. I could make the stitches so they lined up perfectly—each row exactly the same.

Nothing made sense except that I had overstayed my welcome at Linc's place. *It might not be safe for me at home,* I thought, *but I don't feel safe anywhere.* I had to hope that Bert would be satisfied that the cops had Jona—at least for now. And once I was at home, I could find a way to look for the ring.

By then, everyone was milling around the kitchen and stairs like there'd been a gory accident and they all wanted to take a look.

Ashley crouched in front of me. "I'm sorry, Vik. You're our friend." I tried to smile.

Sandy's lecture must even have gotten to Billy. "Friends?" He positioned his hand for a high-five, but I wrapped my arms tighter around my waist. It wasn't that easy. A whole lot more would have to happen before I could be friends with Billy. He dropped his hand, then turned and walked away. Ashley followed.

"I have to go home," I told Linc. It was too late to talk. There was too much chaos in my head for me to know what to do.

When we heard a loud knock on the door, my gut clenched. Linc was ready to jump off the stairs, but Sandy held up her hand to stop him.

"Let's hope it's the cops," she said, her voice tight. She headed through the kitchen, but before she got to the front door it flew open. I could see Bert standing in the doorway, swinging a baseball bat. *Phew,* I thought, *at least no gun.* His hair poked out on the top and sides, making his head look like a dandelion that had gone to seed. He wore flip-flops, long baggy shorts, and a Hawaiian shirt, which would have been comical if I didn't know him.

"Where's that little Jona bastard?" He poked the bat toward Sandy. "I'm gonna kill him when I get my hands on him."

Linc jumped off the stair and ran to his mother's side.

"Don't you be getting all tough with me, Linc. You'll make this worse than it needs to be. Where is he?" Bert was bouncing on the balls of his feet, ready for a fight. "Are you going to give up your little poofy friend?"

Sandy moved into my line of sight so I couldn't see Bert.

"Are you his mother?"

"No. I'm Linc's mom, Sandy Amos. And I'm only going to tell you once, Bert Fromski, to get your sorry ass out of my house. You are not welcome here."

He poked the bat toward Sandy again. Linc reached out to stop him, but Bert swung it at him, just missing his shoulder.

My heart was racing. *Step back, you guys,* I begged silently. *You don't know what he's capable of.*

"Sit down, Linc. Leave this to me," Sandy said. And then she took another step closer to Bert. "We go way back, Bert. I know the sort of guy you are."

Instead of swinging the bat, Bert shuffled his feet, as if he wasn't sure what to do next. I got the feeling that he did remember Sandy. I was still terrified that he would explode and hit her. But I was also stunned at how befuddled he looked.

"Look, mister, nobody barges into my house swinging a bat and talking about my guests like that. I've already told you once, get your ass out of here."

Bert stood there for a few more seconds, swaying on his feet, and then turned toward the porch.

"Whoever do you think you are?" he said, words slurred. He staggered down the front stairs, using the bat like a cane. That's when I realized he was over his limit. Bert was a dangerous drunk until he'd had too much, and then he couldn't connect the dots well enough to follow through on his threats.

Linc shut the door behind him. The house was quiet until we heard the sound of Bert's tires squealing up the road.

"He's drunk," Linc said. "Why didn't we stop him from driving?"

Because you were all too afraid of him, I said to myself. *Now you know how it feels to be me.*

"Fucking white trash," Billy yelled. "He better watch his back."

"Shut up, Billy," Ruby said.

"Ashley," Sandy said, "stop taking pictures and use that thing to call the cops again and tell them about Bert. He shouldn't be on the road."

"I can show them his whole visit on video," she said. "And the cops' visit earlier as well, if you want. Hold on a minute. I'm just posting them. Then I'll call 9-1-1."

"This isn't a damn game," Sandy snapped. "The cops need to pick Bert up."

"Not 9-1-1. Call directly to the station," Ruby said. "But either way, it's not going to do a crapload of good. As long as Bert gets home without killing someone with his car, what are they going to do?"

My muscles hurt when I tried to move. I was relieved Bert hadn't hit anyone, but what would have happened if he had come earlier? What if Jona had been there?

Sandy took the phone from Ashley after she had dialled. "What? Are you telling me that a man can come to my home and threaten a house full of kids with a baseball bat, and now he's driving drunk, and you don't have anyone to protect us? In an hour or so? Yeah. Yeah. I know. Nothing you can do. Right. Yeah, I know how far we are from Simpson Mills."

Sandy came back into the kitchen and collapsed on a chair. "Damn them. Damn Bert and damn this whole frickin' mess." Her hands shook when she picked up her coffee cup.

"It was lucky that he'd had a couple too many," I said.

"Listen to me, honey. Nobody's bluffing when they are

making threats like that." Her voice was trembling. "That man is dangerous, and you need to remember it."

She didn't need to tell me. I knew exactly what it felt like when he swung a bat and when it hit me across the back of my head. I also knew what it felt like when he lied to the doctor and told her that I'd fallen down the stairs. After that, the hospital started a file on me and on Bert. A counsellor told me that they would make sure he didn't get away with it anymore. But that was years ago, and here I was, watching him swinging the same damn bat.

"I've gotta go home," I said. I felt like my life had totally left the tracks. No amount of talking or self-talk or even positive thinking was going to help me now.

Sandy shook her head. "No, honey. You better stay here. That man is dangerous."

"He won't go after me," I said. "He's too drunk now to do any damage. He'll just be sleeping it off."

"You can't go home," Ruby said. "You're not safe. Why don't you come home with me? You can stay at my place for as long as you want."

"Thanks, Ruby, but I can't."

Going home was a chance I needed to take. I needed my blanket, my knitting, and my bedroom, where I could be quiet and think straight. I needed time to figure out how to set things right. I was in too deep now for anybody else to help me.

I watched everyone talking as if there were cartoon speech bubbles coming out of their mouths. I was the only one in the house who knew there was nothing real going on here. Everything from start to finish was a lie. And I was the one responsible for that.

When we heard a car pull into the driveway, Linc got up and peeked through an opening in the blinds. "Vik, it's your mom."

"Check the car," Sandy ordered. "Make sure the old man isn't with her."

Linc took another look. "Can't tell for sure, but I don't see him."

A swoosh of cold air whipped into the room when he opened the door. The sun had gone down, and it felt like rain was on its way.

"Is Victoria here?" Dell asked Linc.

"Yeah, I'm here." I got up and walked toward her.

"I need you to come home." Her voice was low and flat, though it didn't look like Bert had taken the bat to her.

"Isn't it enough for you that they took Jona in?" Billy said. "You want more now?"

Dell looked surprised.

"Vik, you don't have to go," Linc said. "You can stay here with us."

"I better go," I said.

Linc blocked my way when I tried to step around him. "But it's not safe for you to go home."

"Come to my place," Ruby repeated.

Dell flicked her head back, clearly embarrassed. "I don't know what you're talking about. At least at home Vik won't be hanging around with thieves."

"Jona's no thief," Linc said.

"I know you're a good boy, Linc. But be careful about the friends you choose. They can get you into trouble."

It was a rare occurrence when I thought Dell was right. But

this time she was. Linc didn't know it, but his new best friend was ruining his life. Just not in the way Dell thought.

Sandy gave me a hug, looking concerned.

"I'll be fine," I told her.

She looked at Dell. "You better make sure your old man keeps his hands off her."

Dell shot a vicious look back. "It's none of your business what goes on in my family."

"Oh, yes, it is," Sandy said, "and I'll be checking up to make sure Vik is okay."

When you have two choices and neither one is any good, what difference does it make which choice you take? I didn't deserve Sandy's protection, not with the secret I was keeping. I didn't deserve Linc, either, or the life we could have together. Bert and Dell were biology. It was as simple as that.

I gave Linc a quick kiss on his cheek. "I'm not all right, but I'm going home."

Linc

"I just want to make sure Bert isn't waiting in the back seat," Mom said as she peeked between the blinds and watched Dell's car take off.

I was pretty sure Bert wouldn't be hiding in the car. If he'd been with Dell, he'd have been staggering around our house, yelling at everybody and telling Vik what to do.

Mom came over to where I was, shuffled the sofa cushions, and made room between Ruby and me to sit down.

All I wanted to say was *Mom, please tell me that Bert is not going to kill Vik.* And that was just fucked up. How could she know what Bert was capable of doing? So I stayed silent.

After a few minutes I jumped up. "I'm going over there."

Mom gripped my shirt and held on. "No, you're not. What makes you think you can fix this? You could make it worse."

"I need to get Vik out of there."

"She chose to go back," Mom said.

"That doesn't mean it was right."

"I know. But she made the decision."

What if Vik was wrong, though? What if it was the worst decision she ever made in her life?

I made a move to pull away, but Mom held on. "What are you planning to do? Barge into her house and drag her out? Linc, you can't force her."

I grabbed my phone.

Linc to Vik: `Vik, u ok?`

She answered instantly.

Vik to Linc: `Don't worry`

Even though she was probably not home yet, I felt relieved.

"Good," Mom said. "For now, that's all you can do. Stay in touch."

I got up, went into the kitchen, and sat at the table, thinking about Bert at the door with that bat in his hand. It got me wondering what Vik really lived through at home. She'd told me Bert was violent, but I hadn't realized just how bad he was. Maybe I should have, but I didn't.

Ruby came in and sat next to me. "You okay?"

"No. I was going to talk to Vik tonight, just the two of us. I promised her. Then one thing led to another and we didn't get to do it."

"Did she say what she wanted to talk about?"

"No. I can't figure it out. She's been super weird with me lately."

"You worried?"

"Fucking terrified, more like."

"I could go with you to Vik's house. We could persuade her to come back with us," Ruby said.

I heaved a huge sigh. "No. I think Mom's right. Who's to say Bert and Dell would even let her come to the door? We could just make it worse."

"Do you have any idea what's bugging her? I mean, other than this ring business?"

"Not really." But if anyone knew what Vik was thinking, it would be Ruby. "You? Do you know what's bugging her?"

"I'm not sure what the hell happened today. But even before all of this shit, she wasn't liking Jona very much."

"Jesus, everything seems to be about Jona. Jona this. Jona that."

"Maybe that's how Vik feels."

"I don't get it. I thought she liked him."

"She did. But now she thinks you like him."

"I do."

"Linc, you can't be that stupid."

"What the hell do you mean? I've known the guy for a month. I like him. Is there a law against that?"

"Maybe she's worried that you like him too much."

"Oh, come on. That's just weird."

"Maybe it's weird to you, but it's obvious to me. Jona really likes you. And he's the hottest thing going in Carterton—guy or girl."

"So what are you saying?"

"You know what I'm saying."

"No, Ruby, I don't. Stop repeating the same thing. You're starting to sound like Bert."

Ruby didn't rise to the bait. "Think about it from Vik's perspective."

"How the hell do I do that? Vik is making everything so damn complicated! I can't understand her lately. Maybe Bert's gotten to her with his stupid pussy talk about Jona."

"This isn't about Bert. It's about Vik," Ruby said.

I pulled out my phone.

Linc to Vik: Vik u okay? I know we need to talk.

No response. *Don't worry,* I told myself. *She's probably just left her phone in her room or something.*

"Well, if that's what Vik thinks, she's wrong," I said. "Just plain wrong."

"Maybe so. But I'd love Jona to give me as much attention as he gives you."

"You are totally messed up, little cousin. And you are no help at all."

I could hear Mom in the living room on the phone. "This is Sandy Amos again. I also want you to check on Bert Fromski's house. His daughter just went home, and she could be in danger."

She gave them our address and phone number again. She got me thinking, *What if the next thing we see on TV is a crazy shoot-out rampage where some maniac takes out his family? A maniac called Bert Fromski.*

Linc to Vik: `Vik, answer me, babe. This isn't Jona's fault.`

As soon as I pressed *Send*, I thought about what Ruby had said. I wanted to delete the message, but it was too late.

Linc to Vik: `I mean this isn't about Jona. It's about you and me`

Linc to Vik: `I love you`

Jona

By the time Hopper stopped in the parking lot at the station, the stench in the back seat was killing my stomach. When he opened the door, I staggered out, bent over, and puked every last KD noodle into the ditch.

"That was decent of you," the little cop said. "Thanks for sparing the back seat of the cruiser." It was a lame attempt, but at least he was trying to lighten up the situation.

Hopper took a hold of the back of my jacket. "Finished?"

"Yeah." I wiped my mouth with my sleeve. "At least, I think so."

He nudged me from behind toward the station. My stomach churned as I swallowed the rank taste of acid.

Inside, the short cop, Mainwaring, led the way past the receptionist. She nodded at us, as if we were coming in for a friendly visit. I followed the cop down a narrow hall and into a small room with a table and four chairs in the centre. Off to the side there was a counter with a coffee machine and phone. The only window looked back into the hallway.

Hopper shoved me toward the table.

"You don't have to get rough with me. I'll cooperate." I shocked myself by speaking up. "There's been some kind of mistake. I'm sure it'll all get cleared up when we talk."

He leaned over until we were nearly touching nose to nose. "There's been no mistake, John."

"Jona. My name is Jona."

He picked at the end of his nose, as if his nose hairs were irritating him. "Jona, then. Just so you know, we aren't going to have a talk." He flicked his head toward Mainwaring, who had put some papers on the table. "You are going to read those papers and sign them. I am going to ask you questions. And you are going to answer them."

Mainwaring said, "You have the right to have a lawyer or an adult here with you. Or, if you want, you can phone to talk to someone at any time during our conversation. We will be getting in touch with your parents to let them know what's going on."

"No," I said, without thinking what the hell I was saying. "I don't need a lawyer or an adult. I didn't do anything wrong."

"I think we'll find that out for ourselves," Hopper said. "Now up you get. We're going to give you a quick check to see if you were dumb enough to leave the ring on your body."

He checked my jacket and shoes. Thankfully, it was Mainwaring, not Hopper, who patted my shirt pocket and pants. He slipped his fingers around the waist of my jeans and felt my jeans pockets front and back. He did a two-handed rubdown of my socks, both feet, and then stood up. "Nothing there."

"Or here," Hopper said, throwing my jacket on the counter and my shoes under the table.

Mainwaring pointed to the papers. "If you are sure you don't want anyone here, then go ahead and read those. Answer the few questions on them, and we'll need your signature."

God, what was this? A test? There were two pages of tiny print that I could hardly read, let alone understand. It felt like a swarm of bees was buzzing inside my head, and it was all I could do to focus my eyes. I ticked a Yes box for a few things, wrote down my address and Mom's cell number, and signed my name. That much I could comprehend. The rest was a blur. For all I knew, I was signing my life away.

The cops had poured themselves coffee, and Hopper was sauntering around the room, slurping noisily, while I wrote.

"Thanks." Mainwaring took the papers when I was finished and put them on the counter. "Just so you know, this interview will be videotaped. Remember, everything you say can be used as evidence."

Yeah, yeah. I'd heard it all a million times on cop shows. *Focus, Jona,* I told myself. *This is no joke.*

The answers were easy at first. What's your full name? Where do you live? For how long? When did you move to Carterton? Why? Who do you live with?

The questions settled me down. This felt like an exam, and I was pulling one hundred percent.

"Where's your father?"

"Dead."

The thought of my dad choked me up. I couldn't help thinking that maybe it was a good thing the poor guy didn't live long enough to see his son sitting in the cop shop.

"Have you ever been involved with the police?"

My throat closed up and my eyes stung with tears.

"Mr. Prince. Is that a difficult question?"

"No," I said, trying to get my mind off my dad. "I've been to the cop shop—the police station, I mean—in Vancouver a few times, as a witness," I said quickly. Hopper nodded and raised his eyebrows.

"Oh, and I testified in court once after a stabbing incident outside my school. And the cops used to come to George's Basement sometimes, where we played music, so I guess I saw them quite a bit."

Hopper rolled his eyes. "I asked you a simple question: Have *you* ever been involved with the police?"

His eye rolling made me nervous. Was that his plan? Or was I messing up? *Come on, Jona,* I told myself. *Stick to the truth and make it simple.* But my brain seemed to be going numb.

I said, "No." I wanted to tell them I wasn't the kind of guy to mess with the law, and I wanted them to be clear about that. At the same time, it seemed safer to keep my answers short.

"Never?"

"Other than what I told you, no."

Hopper smirked and nodded at Mainwaring. "You heard him. The kid said no."

As Hopper stood and walked to the counter to top up his coffee, an image of Arwen and the BMW flashed into my brain. Was *that* in the files somewhere? Really? But *I* wasn't involved with the police, *she* was. It was a stupid mistake, and everyone knew it.

I was in grade ten. Arwen wasn't even a friend, just someone I knew. Trouble was like oxygen for her. She was a freaking sideshow.

One day she'd said to me, "Bet you don't think I have the balls to steal Mr. Alcock's new BMW."

Alcock was the school principal, but maybe not so smart for someone working in one of the toughest schools in Vancouver. According to Arwen, he left the keys to his car in his office, in a pottery bowl on the corner of his desk.

"Whatever you say, Arwen. But that's just stupid."

"You don't believe me? Just wait." I should have known she meant it, because Arwen was rock hard.

A few days later I was walking home from school when she drove up beside me in a red BMW convertible. "Hop in."

I got in. Yeah. Stupid-ass move. Before I'd even slammed the door, she hit the gas and almost broke my neck from whiplash. She tore along the street like she was driving a racecar. Not even one minute later, cop cars were behind us with their sirens blaring and lights flashing, as if it was a major heist.

"Pull over," I yelled at Arwen.

She stepped harder on the gas.

"Arwen, this is not funny. Pull the fuck over!"

"Pussy."

"Yeah, you're damn right." I was screaming by now. "I'm not into dying."

"Maybe I am!" she said, gripping the wheel and pushing the car even faster.

"Jesus, Arwen!" She was serious. She shot past a city bus, and time slowed way down. "Dying might be fun for you," I said, forcing myself to sound like I wasn't about to crap my pants. "But murdering me is not cool at all."

Maybe she didn't like that idea. Or maybe she didn't really want to die. I don't know, but she slowed down and stopped. Then I found out she wasn't nearly so ballsy as she made out. She turned on the poor little victim routine with the cops and blamed me. The truth eventually came out, but not until they had tried to tag me with being the instigator.

"You mean that thing with the car?" I said to Hopper now. "That wasn't me. I mean, I didn't do anything. I was just in the wrong place at the wrong time. I mean…" I closed my mouth.

Nothing I was going to say would make a difference, and the flashback had messed up my confidence. I swallowed and tried to get my head back on track.

Hopper took a few slurps of his coffee, looking totally pleased with himself. "Where were you today?" he asked. "Retrace your steps. Or were you just in the wrong place at the wrong time—again?"

From then on, every question felt like a trap. I tried to avoid saying anything wrong, instead of just saying what was true. Bad mistake. Even to my ears, everything I said sounded like I was lying.

At some point, Mainwaring started in on me. But if I had to choose, he was a nicer guy for sure. His questions were more straightforward.

"What do you know about the ring?" he began.

"Nothing. I don't know anything about a ring."

"Don't bullshit us," Hopper butted in.

"I'm no bullshitter. I'm telling you the honest-to-god truth. I don't know anything about a ring."

Mainwaring narrowed his eyes, as if that would help him see deeper inside my brain. "Are you telling me that you have never heard anything about the Fromskis' emerald ring?"

"An *emerald* ring?" I tried to fit emeralds into my picture of Vik's place. "Are you saying that Vik's family had an *emerald* ring?"

Hopper butted in again. "We aren't telling you anything. The constable asked you a question."

Mainwaring explained, "Victoria's family owns an heirloom emerald ring, and let's just say it's expensive." He leaned closer to me, with his elbows on the table, and stared into my face.

"I don't know much about the family," I said. "Vik never said anything about a ring. Have you seen their place? It's not the kind of place where, you know, you'd expect to find anything valuable."

Hopper took over again. "What do you know about Linc Amos?"

Linc? Uh-oh. I knew where this conversation might be going. A ring had gone missing from Vik's place. Bert blamed me. But if they couldn't nail me, Linc was going to be the next suspect.

"I've only lived in Carterton since August. I don't know anyone very well."

"But he's your friend?"

"Yeah." I tried not to sound too evasive. "I guess he and Vik are the best friends I have around here."

"Does Linc know about the ring?"

"How should I know?"

"Do you think he could have stolen it?"

"From what I know about Linc, he would not steal anything." I felt myself being pushed farther and farther into a corner. What was this? Flip-a-coin detective work? You've got two choices, Jona or Linc.

"Did I ask you if Linc *would* have stolen a ring?" Hopper was goading me. "I didn't hear that question. Did you, Constable Mainwaring? No, genius, I asked you, *could* he have stolen the ring. And that's different." He leaned back so his chair was balanced on the two back legs. "Let me put it another way. So you can understand. Was there an opportunity for Linc to steal a ring while you were at Victoria's house earlier today?"

I thought back over our visit. I'd already gone over every

detail in my mind, but I'd never thought about how Linc fit into the picture.

"No."

"What makes you so sure?" Hopper asked, his voice harsh.

"I guess I can't say for absolute sure. But other than when I was in the bathroom, Linc was with me and with Vik the whole time we were at Vik's today. Both times."

"And how long were you in the bathroom?"

The answer should have been easy, but how was I going to say I'd hung out for a while to give Linc and Vik time to work out their junk? Hanging out in the bathroom sounded a little kinky.

"I was in there a while. You know." I shrugged. "I don't time myself in the bathroom."

"Well, Jona," Hopper said, "it's either him or you. The ring is gone. Two guys were in the house. Linc Amos and Jona Prince. And it sounds to me like Linc has a full alibi and you don't. Or would you suggest we throw your names in a hat and shuffle them around a bit and pick one?"

It sounded like that was exactly what they were doing, but I thought there was one more name that should be included.

"Vik's dad hates me," I said. "What if he's lying about this just to mess me up?"

Hopper dropped his chair back onto its front legs and slapped his hands on the table. "I don't know about you, Constable Mainwaring, but I think this kid is lying, then trying to pin the blame on his friend, and now he's throwing it right back on the guy who lost the ring. Look, wise guy, we know Linc's never been involved in a theft before. And what do we know about you, genius? First, you and a girlfriend stole a $95,000 BMW, and second, you lied to us about that just now."

He stood up. "We've got enough here, Constable. I'm going to go tell the girls to get a bed ready for this boy. Sergeant Hopper signing out of the interview."

He walked out and left me with Mainwaring. "Tell me," the constable said, "how do *you* think the ring went missing?"

"I don't want to sound disrespectful, but why would someone have a ring like that lying around the house? I don't get it."

He shrugged. "I guess I can say that I wonder the same thing myself."

"Maybe no one stole the ring."

"How do you figure that?"

"Like I said, the old guy could be finding a way to mess me over."

"Not from what I saw," he said. "When we talked to him earlier, he was genuinely upset that his ring was missing."

So much for that theory.

Mainwaring picked up the papers and tossed me my jacket. "Sergeant Hopper will show you to your room," he said and gave me a pat on the back, as if he was doing the good-cop/bad-cop routine.

Hopper, who was standing at the door by then, grabbed my arm and gave me a shove into a room across the hall.

"How long do I have to stay in here?"

"Until someone picks you up," he told me. "Don't worry. We'll have our eye on you." He lifted his head toward the camera in the far corner. Then he snickered and closed the cell door. The latch clunked like I was sealed in a giant vault.

That meant I would be here for a while. Mom was doing an

extra shift at the lodge, so she wouldn't be home till midnight. And she refused to drive in the dark. So once she got the news that I was in jail, and after she had a breakdown about that, I was pretty sure she wouldn't come to pick me up until the morning.

The cell didn't look like it would kill me, but I hated the idea of spending the night in jail. I gave the pillow a few punches to fluff it up, but it stayed rock hard. I lay back and threw my legs onto the cot.

The sickly pale green colour on the walls made me think of the rubber cement I balled up in art class to mimic snot. Besides the cot there was a chair, a table, some magazines, and a buzzer with a sign underneath that read *Attendant.* I looked at the camera and wondered whether to smile or stick my tongue out at it.

I figured the cell was designed to give occupants time to think about their life's mistakes without any distractions, which was the last thing I needed. I had thought enough for one day. I sat up and looked for the light switch...no light switch. I flopped back down on the cot and shut my eyes.

I was dead tired, but how was I going to sleep with my hip bone grinding into this board of a bed? I rolled over on my back, scrunched my jacket up, and stuffed it under my head. But even with my eyes squished shut, the overhead bulb was like headlights blasting in my face. And did anyone think to turn up the heat? I rubbed my hands together to get some circulation in my fingers, then took my jacket out from under my head and covered myself as best I could. I yawned and imagined lying there for a very long night.

Linc

"Finally," Mom said when the cop car pulled into the driveway. "It's about time."

She opened the front door. "Hey, Doug. I'm glad they sent you. Someone who knows the place." She stepped aside to let him in.

I was glad to see Sergeant Firth too. He'd been around the community since I was a kid. He'd helped coach our soccer team in middle school and got along with everyone on the reserve.

He stayed in the doorway. "Hello, Sandy. Linc." He nodded his way around the room to acknowledge everyone. They were all glued to the hockey game. Even Billy didn't look very interested in the cops by this time. "I need to talk to you," he said to me.

"What do you want with him?" Sandy asked.

"I just need to ask him a few questions."

"Then you're not here to talk about Bert?" Her voice rose sharply, the way it always did when she was mad. "Nobody's responded to my calls about the threats he's been making or his drunk driving."

"Sergeant Hopper and Constable Mainwaring did report an altercation at your address. Is that what you're referring to?"

Suddenly Billy got interested and lifted his head. "She's referring to Old Man Fromski coming in here, swinging a bat around, threatening to knock our heads off if we didn't deliver Jona on a platter."

"Needless to say, we've been feeling pretty vulnerable over here," Mom said to Sergeant Firth, her face tight. "It sure would have been nice to see you guys earlier."

"I hear you," he said. "I really do. They've talked to Bert a few times, and apparently he's cooled down. They have his word that he won't come around here again."

"Hah, that's comforting. The one we're really worried about now is Vik," Mom said. "She's gone home, and that could be a bad scene."

"I'm heading over there after I talk to Linc," Sergeant Firth said. "So I'll be checking up on her then."

"Okay. How do we do this?" I asked him. "Want to sit in the kitchen?"

"You okay with the car? It'll be quieter that way." He stepped back outside. "Take your time. I'll wait out here."

"Don't tell him a damn thing," Ruby said. "This is a crock of crap. Someone's doing some bad magic on us, Linc. You should make them get a warrant or something. Isn't that how it works?"

"I'm okay to talk to him. Firth's a good guy. Maybe I can help clear some of this mess up."

"Just be careful, son."

"It's Firth, Mom. How unsafe can it be?" I stuffed my feet into someone's flip-flops.

"I don't mean you're unsafe with Firth. I'm saying this whole case feels like it's trumped up. I don't know what they're up to and I don't like it."

"I'm okay, really." I gave her a quick hug.

"Turn that porch light on. It's dark outside."

Firth opened the police car door and shut it behind me once I was in the passenger seat. Hearing the heavy door slam reminded me of our grade eight soccer team. The year we won the Island pennant. Firth used to make sure Billy and Leon and I had a ride home after the games. We called the cruiser the Ultimate Ride Machine.

He settled in the driver's seat. "What I need from you, Linc, is the straight goods. What happened, when, who was there. That sort of stuff. Don't blow smoke, even if you think something might incriminate you or someone else. It's best to just go with the truth. It works better than trying to cover your ass."

He fiddled around with his tape recorder and blew into the mic a few times, then set it on the console between us.

"Just a few things before I turn this on. You have to trust me on the honesty deal. I've seen innocent people bury themselves by saying what they think I want to hear. Then they tie themselves up in knots trying to get out of what they've said. The old saying really is true: if you tell the truth, you don't have so much to remember."

"But what if I can't remember what happened? It's been crazy around here all afternoon and, to be honest, I'm pretty messed up. I don't know if I can think straight."

"I understand. You'll be fine." He turned on the recorder. "Just answer my questions one at a time, take your time, and be as accurate as possible."

He started by asking about SOS and what we did up on the hill. He asked what I knew about Jona's family and his past. Did I know whether he'd been in trouble with the police before?

What had Jona done at Vik's house that afternoon? Was he ever out of my sight? How long did he spend in the bathroom?

I hated to admit it, but the questions got me wondering if there was something about Jona I didn't know.

"It's not like I interviewed Jona before becoming his friend."

"Of course. Don't worry. You're doing fine." Then he asked, "Are Victoria and Jona friends?"

I took a moment to answer and then spoke slowly. "I thought she liked him. But now I'm not sure. I don't even know if she likes me all that much. I'm having trouble getting the girlfriend thing all figured out."

Firth looked sympathetic. "Did you go to Victoria's house before heading up the mountain?"

"No. But we went straight there afterward."

"You didn't go home first?"

"No."

"Why not?"

Then I remembered that it was Jona's suggestion that we surprise Vik. But I didn't want to say so.

"I knew Vik would want to see us. What we were doing with SOS meant everything to her." I was quiet for a few seconds. Actually, Vik probably hadn't wanted to see the two of us. She had probably wanted to see me. Alone.

Firth seemed to sense that I wasn't sure. "Do you have any more you want to say about that?"

"No. Just that we only stayed a few minutes and then we headed home to change out of our wet boxers. We went back to Vik's house about half an hour later."

I told Firth about what happened when Bert and Dell got home. "Bert was mad as hell."

"What did he say?"

I told him what I could remember. But I couldn't stop thinking that it had been a mistake taking Jona to Vik's.

"The thing is, Bert hates Jona," I said. "It's not only that he's First Nations. Bert thinks he's gay."

"Is he?"

"Is he what?"

"Gay."

God, not him as well. "What difference does it make?"

"To me, none. To the case, relationships often make a lot of difference."

"How the hell should I know? Jona's my friend. He's from Vancouver. He doesn't look like Carterton. He wears purple running shoes. Does that make him gay? I don't think he's ever had a girlfriend. But I don't see what that has to do with anything. He thinks girls are way too complicated."

Firth laughed.

It made me think about what Ruby had said. *Was* Jona gay?

Then I got worried about the way Firth had said "relationships."

"Jona and I aren't in a relationship. We're friends."

"Yeah. I hear you."

But I didn't think he did. "I mean, two guys can just be friends, right?" But that made it sound even worse, so I shut up.

Firth turned off the tape recorder. "How about we take a break?"

"Good idea." I was worried. What had seemed so straightforward before was now messed up. Did I even know anything about Jona?

Firth said, "I've got a few messages to send. You can step outside for a breather if you want."

It took a few seconds for my eyes to adjust to the darkness. I looked at the faint outline of the mountains and remembered jumping in the pool with Jona up at the stream. Was I stupid, like Ruby had said? Did Jona *like* me? Who the fuck cared? I liked the guy and I wasn't gay, so what? I sucked in a big breath, and I could smell the fog rolling in from the ocean.

I was stretching my arms over my head, wishing I was on the beach, when Firth opened his door. "I'm ready when you are." I got back in the cruiser.

His next set of questions was more about me than about Jona. Had I gone to the bathroom while we were at Vik's? (No.) Was Vik with me the whole time? (Yes.) Did I know about the ring? (Yes.) Had I ever seen it? (No.)

Holy crap. I'd been so damn worried about Jona that I hadn't realized the whole fucking mess could do an about-face and be staring down my throat. I wasn't just stupid. I was an imbecile.

"So are you saying I'm a suspect?"

"No," Firth said, with a technically-not-right-now tone to his voice. "But the ring went missing while you and Jona were there, so, for now, there are only two possibilities." He paused for a moment. "You would have had plenty of opportunities to steal the ring in the past if you'd known about it. Better opportunities than today. Unless you were trying to frame your friend, there would be no reason to steal it this afternoon and leave such an obvious trail."

Was he trying to trap me? But Firth wasn't like that. He was a straight shooter, a friend.

Who was I kidding? He was a cop.

"Why would I want to frame Jona?"

"I don't know."

"So then why aren't I the main suspect?"

"Two reasons: supposedly we have an eyewitness. Bert saw Jona coming out of the bedroom when he opened the front door to his house. It sounded like he caught him red-handed, so the police came out and picked Jona up. They didn't want him to have time to hawk the ring."

"You've been to their house, though," I said to Firth. "You know that if Bert was at the front door, he couldn't have seen Jona coming out of the bedroom. You can't see the bedroom door from the front door. Plus, I was there. Bert didn't say anything about a ring."

Firth nodded slowly.

"Did you guys botch this one or what?" I couldn't keep the anger out of my voice.

Firth looked annoyed. "We're checking out Bert's story. And Jona could have headed to Vancouver right away. It's a big city. He could know people there who would buy an expensive ring."

He was right. What did I know about Jona, anyway? Or Vancouver? Or fencing rings? It wasn't an outrageous theory.

"We have to follow certain procedures in these cases," Firth continued. "What we do know is that there's a very expensive ring missing, and it went missing while you and Jona were in the house. You explain it to me. That's why I'm here. To get answers."

If he wanted answers, I was the wrong guy to ask. I had more questions than he did.

"What is the other reason Jona's the prime suspect and not me?"

"You seem to have a pretty tight alibi. From what I can tell, you were with Vik the whole time. Jona was alone long enough to take the ring."

"That's a relief, but why are we the only two suspects?"

"Who else do you think would steal the ring?"

"You were the one who talked about framing. The obvious guy who comes to my mind is Bert."

"Explain."

"He hates me being Vik's boyfriend, and he hates Jona even more. What better way of nailing us both than trumping up this theft? He could be concocting the whole story."

I hadn't thought about the idea beforehand, but once I started, it sounded better and better.

Firth looked interested. "Do you think Dell would be in on it?"

I didn't want to believe that Dell would frame us. Some people are, on some really fundamental level, just bad asses. And there was no doubt that Bert was one of those people. Although Dell was married to him, I didn't think she was bad. I got the impression that, deep down, she was a good person.

"No. Dell wouldn't do that, I don't think. After what's happened today, though, I'm not sure of anything."

"I hear you. We're trying to cover all the bases," Firth said. "For now, Victoria's father is not a suspect. I appreciate you being honest with me, though."

"I didn't steal the ring," I said. "And honestly, I don't think Jona did either."

Vik

"Thanks for coming with me," Dell said. She had an edge of fear in her voice that I'd heard before. She drove slowly, and I had the sense she didn't want to get home any more than I did.

"Did I have a choice?"

She put her hand on my seat so that her fingers touched my leg, and I felt her trembling. Her ragged fingernails didn't match her thin, elegant hands. I glanced over at her and could see a hint of a young woman. But lines had formed around her eyes and lips, making her look permanently tired and unhappy. Her hair was pulled back in a stringy ponytail. She was wearing a stained T-shirt, worn-out sweatpants, and old, scuffed running shoes. Didn't she know how bad she looked? Didn't she care?

I didn't want her to know I was looking at her, so I turned my head, but I did want to pick up her hand. It had been at least five years since the last time I held her hand, back before the mill closed down, when Dell and I spent time together without Bert. She used to hold my hand when we walked to the store to buy ice cream sandwiches.

"Bert's furious," she said. "I don't know what to do with him. He says he'll kill that kid if the law doesn't charge him. He might be all drunked up tonight, but he'll be back at it tomorrow, and he'll be after that kid whenever he gets out. And if we don't get the ring back..." She left the thought hanging.

I thought about saying *Mom*. And telling her the truth. But I got a lump in my throat and my eyes filled up with tears when I thought about how much I needed a mom. Maybe it wasn't Linc or Ruby or Sandy I needed to tell the truth to. Maybe it was Dell.

"I've never liked that Jona fellow, from the first time I saw him. You know what Bert thinks?" Her voice deepened, and any trace of my young mom disappeared. "He thinks Jona, you know...Bert saw Linc and him at TJ's together"—she tightened her lips and nodded—"and just the other day at the gas station, too, looking pretty tight." She spit the words out in a half whisper, as if she was telling me a secret. "You know what I mean?"

"No, Dell, I don't know what you mean."

"You know. Guys and guys." She clamped her lips together and nodded like it was God's truth.

"Geez, Dell, it's the twenty-first century," I told her. Tears burned my eyes. What would Bert say if he'd seen them dancing together the first freaking day they met? Yeah, Jona probably was gay. Whatever. But even so, he couldn't make Linc change. Not like that. Could he? I wanted more than anything to be able to talk to Dell, tell her everything, but I knew now that wasn't going to happen. "Just say the word. Gay, Dell, you think Jona's gay. That he screws other guys."

"Vik! That's gross." Her voice got a couple of notches louder.

"Well, you think you know everything," I yelled. "I'm just spelling it out for you 'cause you think you're so smart."

"You don't have to go all ballistic on me. You're getting more like Bert every day," she shouted back. "I say one thing to you and you're going to bite my head off."

I quit yelling. She was right. I was on the verge of losing it entirely, and no one hated how much I sounded like Bert more than I did. "Let's go inside and get this over with," I said calmly.

When Dell opened the door, Bert was leaning against the wall, holding a beer. His red-faced, glassy-eyed look told me he'd had a few more beers since he was at Linc's.

"Firth's coming over, girl. He's gonna talk to you." His feet shuffled behind me as I walked down the hall. "And you better goddamn well tell him the truth."

"Or what will you do, Bert? Beat me with your baseball bat?"

I went into the bathroom and locked the door.

"All those goddamn cops do is protect the goddamn criminals. You gotta tell 'em, Vik."

It sounded like he was talking right into the crack in the door. He was probably going to crash inside any minute.

"Get the hell away from the door. You are disgusting."

"You know what that little scum will steal next, girl," he taunted me.

"Shut up, Bert," I screamed.

"Linc and Jona, sitting in a tree..."

"Shut the freaking hell up!"

"Vik, calm down," Dell said.

"Get him away from the door."

He didn't shut up, but his voice came from farther down the hall, and then it sounded like he was in the living room. He hollered, "She knows I'm right. That's why she's so goddamn mad."

I opened the bathroom door and peeked out.

By the time I was in my room, Dell was standing in the doorway. It was part of her disaster control strategy—make sure I was out of the way when Bert was on a rampage; then make Bert happy, whatever it took.

"This isn't a good time to get him riled up. He's already fit to explode."

His voice, softer now, resigned, came from the other room. "We are ruined, Delly." Then it changed back to anger. "Dell, where are you? Get in here."

She turned and ran back to the living room.

I shut the door, arranged my pillows against the headboard, put in my earbuds, covered my legs with my blankie, and picked up my knitting. Then I breathed in, one two three four, and out, one two three four. After I found my spot in my knitting, I wound the wool around the needle and pushed the stitch off. One stitch at a time. Round after round. After a few rounds, I calmed down and started to feel in control again.

Just answer Firth's questions, I told myself, *no more, no less.* But I was nervous. *What if I have no choice but to tell the truth? Then what?*

Fourteen rows later, the doorbell clanged in the hall. I put my knitting down, turned the music off, and opened my door a crack.

"It's about time," Bert hollered. "Where were you? Babysitting your little criminal?"

I didn't hear what Sergeant Firth said. But I could hear Dell's little-girl voice trying to calm Bert down.

"Don't 'hush now' me, Dell. Vik'll tell him the truth so he can get on with his job of putting the little scum away."

Firth's voice was firm and loud enough for me to hear him say something about wanting to talk to Bert first.

"I told you on the phone. The ring's gone. The fucking green velvet's lying there, spread-eagle, in the jewellery box with nothing on top. You know what I mean. Yeah, you do."

He stopped talking, and I got the feeling that he was sloppy drunk and not much use to Firth.

Then he blurted out, "I'm telling you, I saw that little creep, Jona, red-handed. You should have seen the guilty look on his face when he was running from the bedroom back into the kitchen. I didn't know what he was up to at the time. Now I do, don't I."

"I have just a few questions about the ring," Firth said. "Maybe as much for Dell as you."

"Don't you be getting Delly into this. She's already out of her mind, poor thing."

"Here," Firth said. "I'll just put my tape recorder here on the coffee table, if you don't mind."

"Yeah, I mind," Bert said. "But you're the cop."

"First of all," Firth said, "who owns the ring?"

I stepped out of my bedroom and tiptoed along the hall toward the living room to make sure I didn't miss anything. No one answered. I imagined Bert and Dell shooting looks back and forth. I'd never thought about whether there were official ownership papers or something for a ring.

"It was left to me, Delphine Buckingham, in my mother's will," Dell said so quietly that I almost couldn't hear.

"Well, yeah," Bert said. "She's the one that got the papers. I guess it's the old lady's will you want to be looking at. Ain't that so, doll?"

Firth said, "That might work. And who holds the insurance for the ring?"

There was another silence, longer this time.

Dell finally said, "The ring isn't insured."

I crept forward until I could see into the living room.

"So the ring is not insured at all? What about your house insurance?"

"You heard the woman," Bert shouted. "We don't take that shit. Not on the ring, the house, or my own fucking ass. We don't owe nobody nothing, and we don't pay nobody nothing. Insurance companies are nothing but money-grubbing pirates." Given how drunk I figured he was, he surprised me by how coherently he was still able to talk. "They take you for all you've got, promising this and that to protect you. Then you read the small print and you get nothing. You think I'm stupid enough to give those thieves my money? The goddamn police can't even protect us. Sure as hell insurance companies won't."

"So, no contents insurance," Firth said.

It was quiet long enough for Bert to catch on to why Firth was asking about insurance.

"Oh, oh, so I know what you're up to." Then he broke into a coughing fit that sounded like he was going to spit up his lungs.

"This isn't a good time for him," Dell said. She was patting Bert's arm. "He's not feeling well enough for all these questions."

"Like hell." He caught his breath and pushed her hand away. "Here's where the cops want to blame the victim. Instead of getting out there and finding my ring and catching the thief, you're sitting here in my house, asking me whether or not I'm up to some kind of dirty little scheme."

Firth said, "It's standard procedure, Bert. I've got to ask the questions. I don't mind taking Dell aside. These are questions for her as much as you if she's the owner of the ring."

"I didn't steal my own goddamn ring, you fucking moron!"

"Bert, I have to warn you—" Firth's voice didn't get louder, but he spoke more forcefully.

"Fucking don't warn me," Bert interrupted. "I'm warning *you*. I'll take you and your whole goddamn police force down."

Dell said, "Calm down, Bert. Of course he has to ask those questions. It's just procedure."

"Yeah, well, he's not asking me another goddamned thing in my house."

Firth said, "I'll see what I can do with what you've told me. Now I need to ask Victoria a few questions."

I stepped into the living room.

"How about we talk in the car?" he said when he saw me.

"You tell him what that faggot friend of yours did!" Bert yelled after us as we went outside.

My whole body shook when Sergeant Firth shut the car door and settled into the driver's seat.

"I'm sorry." I tried to keep my jaw still so my teeth wouldn't chatter. "If I look scared, it's because it's been a crazy scene around the house."

"I understand. Just breathe deeply and take your time. Just tell me what you know and you'll be fine."

Just don't lie to him, Vik, I told myself. *Police get super pissed when you lie to them. No one says you have to tell him everything you know—less is more.* But that was how I got into this situation in the first place, by not telling people everything I knew.

And up until then I hadn't lied. I just hadn't had the courage to tell the truth.

Firth's face was pale, and his movements were quick and jumpy, like he was tired or in a hurry, which didn't exactly make me feel comfortable.

"This will only take a few minutes," he said, turning on his tape recorder. "I just want you to tell me what happened this afternoon when Linc and Jona came over."

The details were easy—Linc's phone call, the KD, Jona's trip to the bathroom.

"How long was Jona in the bathroom?"

"Oh, I'd say five minutes."

"Really?"

"I don't actually know how long five minutes is, so I'm not sure. It was quite a long time."

"What sort of mood was he in when he came out?"

"I don't know." Then I realized what he was getting at, and it made me wonder if I should say his mood had changed—that he was agitated. But I stuck to the exact truth. "The same as when he went in, I guess."

"And what about Linc? Did he go into the bathroom?"

"No."

"Were you with him the whole time?"

Oh. My. God. Is Linc a suspect? Why didn't I think of that?

"Yes. Yes, for sure." I tried to calm down. But I couldn't help thinking about everything I'd said up until then. Had anything implicated Linc? How could he possibly think Linc could do such a thing?

"Every minute," I said. "Linc didn't go anywhere at all."

He didn't ask me if I thought Jona stole the ring or if I had any ideas about where the ring might be. He didn't even ask me if I thought Bert was covering something up. Mistake. The truth was, Firth didn't do a very good job. Because if he had asked those questions, who knows what I would have told him.

"That's enough for tonight," he said. "If I need more, I'll get back to you."

I opened the car door. “Okay,” I said and gave the door a shove. “You know where I’ll be.”

He gave me a little finger wave and sympathetic smile as if to say *You poor pathetic you.*

Jona

I thought I'd never get to sleep on that uncomfortable cot. Then, what seemed like a split second later, I was startled out of sleep by the sound of the metal latch clicking and the door creaking open. I sat bolt upright and found myself facing a cop who had pulled up the chair and sat down next to me.

"Jona? I'm Sergeant Firth. Your ride is here."

"Oh, no." I wasn't ready to face Mom. "I mean, what time is it?"

"Eleven-thirty."

I shook my head to get the fog out. *How could Mom be here already?*

"You are free to leave." There was something about the guy that I liked right away. "But don't be taking any trips to Mexico. This case isn't over. The allegations against you are serious, and you're still being investigated. So it's important that you don't disappear."

"I won't be going anywhere."

"You ready?"

"I guess so."

Ready or not, there wasn't much I could do but follow him into the hall. And, innocent or not, I had the length of the hall to prepare for whatever Mom was going to throw at me. I couldn't blame her; picking your kid up at the cop shop must be low on a mom's list of favourite things to do. The added problem was that this episode was a major turnaround in the story of our lives; right here was where the lyrics did a hairpin turn. Mom had never done mom sort of things, and this was a hell of a way to start.

Jail, bail,
my boy's a failure to sail,
he's lost the trail...

It sounded like a bad country song.

I took a long breath. When we passed the receptionist, she handed me my wallet and cell phone. We turned the corner, and Sandy Amos shot forward and threw her arms around me.

"Jona, I'm sorry it took me so long to get here. You must be starving." She held my hand like I was a little kid. "I've got something for you to eat in the car."

"You guys take care," Firth said.

She sighed out loud when we stepped through the door. "Phew. I'm glad that's over with."

"Why do people say junk like that?" I asked when we were in the car.

"Like what?"

"Like, 'you guys take care.' That statement has absolutely no meaning, it's a garbage statement, and I'm fucking tired of hearing shit like that. Do you really think he gives a fuck whether we take care or not?"

"Wow, buddy. You've come out of there mean and fighting!"

I laughed. "Sorry. What I really mean is, thank you so much for coming to pick me up. And I'm happier than hell that I didn't have to face Mom in that waiting room."

"You'll face her soon enough," Sandy said as she dug her

hand into a bag in the back seat. "I called the station and finally got to talk to Hopper—asshole—but he did say that I could come and get you."

She handed me a sandwich wrapped in wax paper, and a stack of cookies wrapped the same way. It looked like the lunches Linc brought to school. They screamed "Mom makes my lunch," and they looked gourmet compared to my shrink-wrapped, manufactured lunches. I unwrapped the sandwich and took a bite.

"You're right. I'm starving."

Sandy reached across the console and gave me an awkward sideways hug. "So, are you free?"

"Not exactly." I told her what the cop had said. "But after all that, they don't know what the hell really happened."

"Linc thinks Bert should be a suspect," she said.

"I told the cops the same thing."

"Look at me, Jona, and tell me something." She turned a full ninety degrees and faced me. "Did you steal the ring?"

"No." What more could I say? "I did not steal the ring."

She looked back at the road.

"Good." She took quite a while to ask, "Then who did?"

"That's the million-dollar question. All I know is that I didn't steal a ring. I'm not a thief. And I'm not a liar."

She took another look at me. "That means someone else is."

"I hope it's not up to me to figure that one out," I said. I knew everyone was thinking that if I was not the thief, it must be Linc, and my guess was that she knew this.

I opened the bundle of cookies. "Want one?"

"Yeah." She smiled. "At least one. That's why I packed so many."

We drove without saying a word until we had finished the cookies.

"Bert terrifies me," I told her.

"That's because he's a bad guy. I always try to see good in people, but no matter how hard I look, I can't find any good in him. Is that possible?"

"You know him?"

"I knew Bert at school, and my parents knew his dad. His family was one of the first white families to settle in the area, so we go way back, before I was even born."

"Wow, that is an exceptional thought." In Vancouver, almost everybody I knew had come from somewhere else. The idea that families lived together for generations—or lived just across the bridge—and still hardly knew each other seemed strange to me.

"I don't know too much about his family, but he's been an asshole for as long as I can remember. He hung around with a group of boys that called themselves the Hound Dogs. They were stupid, but they were also seriously mean. They cruised around Carterton in an old van and randomly beat up our guys from the reserve. And you don't want to know what they did to the girls. I was lucky, I guess. They roughed me up a couple of times, but they never really got their hands on me."

I didn't want to ask what she meant by "roughed me up," and she didn't tell me, so I pushed on.

"Does he know Linc's your son?"

"He put it together when he saw me this evening. But he was staggering around too much to make anything of it. I've always worried about Vik, but I've tried not to say too much. I figure she should have a chance to create her own life. But you know what?" Sandy asked the question as if she were chatting with her best friend. "It's almost too weird for words."

I said, "What?" as if she was about to tell me some excellent gossip.

"Hopper's a new cop around here. But when I first saw him, I thought I recognized him, and I got the feeling that he thought the same about me. Now I think I know why. He was one of those damn Hound Dogs—as bad as Bert or worse."

"I believe it. He seems seriously mean too." I shuddered. "This place freaks me out."

I knew immediately that what I'd said wasn't exactly true.

"Actually, earlier today I was in love with this place. Now, all of a sudden, Carterton terrifies me. I get the feeling there are monsters walking around."

"It's the same place. It doesn't mean you can't love it just because now you've seen some of our bad guys."

At that instant, rain started pelting down so hard it sounded like someone was using drumsticks on the roof of the car. The rain and the squeaky windshield wipers made it hard to hear what Sandy was saying.

"But I know what you mean. Those guys still have a special hate for First Nations."

"And a double hate for me."

"What do you mean?"

I knew what I meant, but I wasn't sure I wanted to talk about it. Should I say they hated gays? But I'd never thought of myself as gay. I'd never had to, because in Vancouver I looked normal. No one asked me if I was gay just because I had a ponytail and wore cardigans and coloured shoes.

I faked a laugh. "Bert calls me some stupid stuff like poof and faggot and homo. I mean, really, who uses those words these days?"

I tried to sound like I wasn't bothered, but the truth was that the words scared me. I looked straight ahead to avoid her reaction. But I could see out of the corner of my eye that she had turned and was staring at me.

"Well," she said, as if she was going to make an announcement. "Are you?"

"Am I what?"

And I realized she was asking the big question—the one I had never been asked. The one that I didn't know how to answer.

"Are you in love with Linc?"

Without thinking I said, "No." And then more words tumbled out of my mouth. "I didn't think that I would find a friend in a redneck town like Carterton. Linc's just a super great guy."

Love Linc? I threw the idea around a few times. It didn't make sense. At least not *love* love. But when I started thinking about love and about Linc, all I could do was picture him standing in his boxers up at the stream.

Trying to get rid of the Linc thoughts, I told Sandy, "I was attracted to Vik when I first met her. I was kind of disappointed when she mentioned she had a boyfriend."

"Really?" she said, as if she was relieved. "I guess people around here aren't used to the way you look. It's probably a small town/big town thing. And then they think it's gay."

Gradually the air outside got so dense with fog that Sandy had to slow down to a crawl. It felt like the two of us were buried in a time capsule and that the world was turning somewhere outside without us.

"So you aren't gay?"

I took a long, deep breath and exhaled slowly. I said to myself, *My name is Jona Prince. I'm sixteen years old. I have a slight build. I have fine features like Michael Jackson after his surgeries. I have almost waist-length black hair. I wear skinny jeans, coloured high-tops, button-up shirts, and cardigans. I am the son of a messed-up single mom, and my dad's dead. I'm smart not tough. Artistic not athletic. Funny not aggressive. I think girls are beautiful, just not very interesting. I think boys are stunning but sort of scary. When I think about sex, I get hard and more than a little worried. I haven't done the act yet and I'm not sure I'll be any good at it. The truth is that I have only started thinking about sex since I got to Carterton, and now that I've started, I can't stop. But if the question is do I think about having sex with boys more than I think about having sex with girls, I guess the answer would be yes. Does that make me gay?*

I said, "I don't know."

Sandy began laughing so hard she was shaking. "That's the best answer. A kid who really understands sex." She kept laughing. "He says, I don't know."

I wasn't sure whether I should be offended. But then she said, "Really, Jona, I'm serious. That's the only right answer for a lot of sixteen-year-olds. And that's okay. It's okay with me."

A few minutes out of Carterton, she asked, "Do you want to go home or to our place?"

"I'd love to postpone the inevitable, but Mom will be home, and I have to fill her in sometime."

We pulled in and parked by the trailer. Mom had a candle burning in the living room. It was casting a dim yellow light through the tiny windows and made the place look like it was part of a fairy tale.

Sandy picked up my hand and squeezed it till it hurt. "Call if you need anything."

Linc

I couldn't focus on the screen. I pushed away from the computer and flopped on my bed. The noise from the game played background to Firth's questions, which were running through my head on an endless loop.

What the fuck? I had gone from being totally innocent—the guy who was worrying about Vik and Jona—to one of the main suspects.

Just tell the truth, Firth says. Oh yeah, I was thinking, that should be easy. And then I start making shit up to cover for Jona. What the hell was I thinking?

Why was I covering for him? Maybe he did steal the ring. I wasn't with him every minute. And, Jesus, did Firth really think that I had secretly planned to steal the ring all along, and that I waited until Jona was in the house so I could frame him? Who would think of shit like that? If it weren't for my alibi, if Vik hadn't been with me every second I was at her place, they'd probably think that Jona was innocent and I was the guilty one.

There was no way I was going to get to sleep.

"Hey, Linc," Mom called. "Jona's out. I just got home."

I had wanted to go pick him up, but Mom said she didn't want me anywhere near the cop shop. Which made me wonder if she was thinking the same as Firth and the others, and that maybe I was not out of the woods.

I threw on a pair of shorts and opened the door.

"He okay?"

"Yeah. He's fine." She stepped into my bedroom. "At least, he's out."

"For good?"

"For now. He doesn't know what's going to happen."

I thought, *Join the club.*

"You want to talk?" Mom asked.

"Not really. I just want the day to be over."

"I hear you. What about Vik? She okay?"

"Yeah. She seems okay."

"It's after one. It's time to put this day to rest." She turned to the door and said over her shoulder, "Everything's going to be okay."

Hah! Yesterday I would have believed her. "How do you figure?"

"Because the truth will show up."

"The truth? What the hell is the truth?"

"What really happened to the ring," she said, and I was wishing hard that she was right. "There's a whole other story we haven't heard yet."

"Like what?" I wanted her to tell me something that I *could* believe.

"If I knew, I'd tell you. The only thing I know for sure is that we have to wait. No matter how painful it is."

"Great. That doesn't sound okay to me."

"It's the hard parts that make you strong. Isn't that what the old people used to say?" She kissed my forehead. "Good night."

"Good night."

Jona

I took my time walking along the overgrown driveway toward the porch. The fog covered the house like soup poured in a bowl. It wasn't raining anymore, but it was doing a weird west coast thing where the air smelled and almost tasted like water. I breathed in and shivered. There was no easy way to tell Mom.

Through the window, I could see Mom's flickering silhouette. It looked like she was asleep in her chair with a book on her lap, a shawl around her shoulders, and a pop can on the coffee table. I thought about the moment, earlier that day, when I'd jumped in the stream, and figured I should take the same approach here. Make a run for it, the quicker the better, and get it over with.

I took a breath and turned the doorknob, then yanked the door open with both hands, making a loud grinding sound.

"Jonsey." Mom sat up and held her hands out toward me. In normal families, her actions would have meant she wanted a hug. But in our family it meant she wanted me to hold her hands for a second. It was a greeting she had devised that allowed her to avoid any chance of body contact. Hugging was only on the menu in our house when Aunt Lonnie was visiting. And even then, Mom didn't partake.

I did the obligatory thing and grabbed her hands, one in each of mine. I squeezed them a couple of extra times, then sat on the loveseat across from her, leaned in closely so we were almost knee to knee, and looked at her. I mean I looked at her properly. For the first time in my life I looked at her like I was an adult and she was an adult. She was so small, she would have had to stretch to touch the floor with her toes. Her face was pale and tired, and her makeup was smudged around her eyes. Her hair was tied up in a loose knot, and wisps hung freely around her face. She wore pearl earrings and a gold chain around her neck. I had never seen her in jewellery or makeup, and, Jesus, when did she get so pretty?

"Mom," I said, "did you get any messages on your cell?"

"I don't know." She started looking around for her phone. "I haven't turned it on since before work."

"Never mind." I took a deep breath. "I just got out of jail. Vik's parents are accusing me of stealing a super-expensive emerald ring. I didn't do it, but I'm in deep shit."

I was speaking to her, but it was as if the words turned around and came at me like a freight train. Suddenly I really understood how deep the shit was. Until then I'd been going through the motions—the cop car, the interview, the jail cell. The one-thing-at-a-time approach had got me lost in the trees and had hidden the forest. Was that how the saying went?

Mom frowned. "Say that again."

"I just got out of jail. What the hell would I do with an emerald ring?"

She puckered her mouth and shook her head slowly, as if she were trying to shake loose her confusion. She took a mouthful of pop, contorted her face like she was downing cough medicine, and took a noisy swallow.

"Maybe you could sell it," she said.

Did she think this was a joke?

"What the hell would you say something like that for?"

"You asked what you'd do with a valuable ring. I'm just saying that one thing you could do with it is sell it."

Now I was the one who was confused. But there was something I liked about her answer, and I laughed. She laughed as well, although clearly neither of us thought it was funny.

"I didn't steal the ring, Mom. They are trying to frame me."

"I hear you. I hear you." I noticed that she didn't say she believed me.

I told her every detail of my day, and an amazing thing happened. She listened like she was the parent and I was the kid. She said things like "Why did you go over to the girl's house in the first place? You knew that man was a monster." Which was a perfectly reasonable, motherly sort of question.

"Linc said it would be okay."

"Do you do everything Linc says?"

What? Was *she* interrogating me now? I wasn't sure I liked this new relationship of ours.

By the time I finished talking, my day sounded crazier than fiction, even to me. "Wow. I can hardly believe all that happened to me."

"I believe you," she said. "No one could make up a story like that."

She leaned back in her chair and looked at my face as if she was studying each feature.

"So," she said. She put her hand up to her mouth and took a long pause. "Who stole the ring?"

"How should I know?"

"Did Linc steal it?"

"No way. Why would he pick today to steal the ring? He could have done it anytime."

"But he didn't have such a good cover as he had today. Maybe Vik and him are in it together." She furrowed her brow as if she didn't like what she'd said any better than I did. "Are they framing you?"

"Really?" I was exasperated. "You sound as bad as the cops."

"So you don't like my ideas? You have anything better?" She took another swig of pop, followed by the same contorted face and gigantic swallowing ordeal as before.

"Why do you drink pop like that? I know it's a little off the topic, but if it's so hard for you to swallow, why not just sip it or drink juice or something?"

"Good idea." She laughed. Then she took another big swig.

I started laughing, and soon we were full belly-laughing together, so hard that she almost spit the pop in my face.

"Settle down," I said, but we couldn't stop. We giggled like little kids until my stomach hurt.

"Getting back to the problem," I said. "I wouldn't throw the best friend I've ever had under the bus. So what I'm saying is, I'm not going there, and Linc did not steal the ring, period."

"Okay," she said and nodded.

"The truth is, Mom..." I started to laugh again.

"I'm waiting. Seriously, I want to know what the truth is." She reached out and took my hands in hers. Her hands were warm and soft, and her spindly fingers had a surprisingly firm grasp. She gently massaged my fingers with hers.

"I don't know what the truth is. I don't even know who the hell I am. All I can say is I'm Jona Prince and I live down the road from the reserve in Bill's old broken-down two-bedroom trailer that doesn't even have a door that opens properly. And I know that if there's a fire, we're screwed, because the trailer doesn't have any other door that opens either.

"Just a sidebar, Mom. Did you know I lie awake at night, worried about how we're going to escape a fire?"

"No, I didn't know you worried about it. But I worry about it as well."

"Commitment?" I said. "That you will tell Bill the door needs to be fixed?"

"Commitment," she said. "Now, back to what you know is true."

"Well, I've lived in Vancouver all my life, and now I live in Carterton. I have a grandmother somewhere in Winnipeg who doesn't want to see me, an aunt in Toronto who buys me fabulous clothes and shoes and everything else a guy could want. I have a dead dad, from cancer, but I'm not allowed to say the C word or my mom will freak." She didn't even twitch. So I said the word again. "Cancer." She kept her eyes fixed on me. "I have a Mohawk family who probably doesn't know I exist. I have a kid mother who's been my best friend and psycho patient, and now she has work and is doing a great job starting her life over. And that is all I know for sure about anything."

She let go of my hands and straightened her back. "That's it?"

"That's it."

We both leaned back in our chairs.

"Oh, yeah," I said. "There is one more thing."

"That was enough, don't you think?"

"No. One more thing. I did not steal that ring."

"Jona," Mom said, with a different tone than earlier, "I have one more thing as well. Or maybe two or three."

She looked at me and didn't say anything for a few minutes. Then, instead of talking, she got up and went into the bathroom. When she came out, her hair was wet around the edges and the makeup smudges had disappeared.

"There's something you don't know, and now is as good a time as any to tell you." She didn't sit back down. She paced around the room, which in reality meant she was making very small circles around the coffee table.

"What don't I know?"

"You don't know about cancer. You don't know about your dad. And you don't know about your Mohawk family."

I started to laugh, thinking she must be kidding. How could she have made up a list like that?

I said, "You said the C word. Don't you remember it's not allowed in our house? Your rule."

She nodded. "It seems like truth and lies are the subject tonight, so I have to tell you a couple of my own. But before you think that I've got a new brave streak because of the crap you're in...or in case you think that now I'm going to do the right thing because I've found a previously unknown source of adultness..." She laughed. "Forget that. I'm still the spineless Carmen I've always been. It's just that, right now, I have no choice. I'm being forced to turn some of my lies into truths."

By then, I had flutterings in my stomach that felt like an eagle flapping its wings.

"I don't like to admit it, but the only reason I'm telling you this stuff now is because I got a phone call last week from your grandma in Ontario. She said she's not got long to live, and she wants to see you. She also said that it's about time I let your dad see you as well."

Her words about my grandmother turned into mumbo-jumbo when I tried to make sense out of them. But the thing about letting Dad see me was clear as glass. I just didn't know what the hell she was talking about.

"Dad?" I finally choked the word out.

"I have no choice. It's grow-up time for me. And it's time for you to know the real story about who you are."

"So tell me." Blood was pounding through my veins. "What the hell do you mean, allow my dad to see me?"

"Shhh, Jona." She flapped her hands like she was telling me to sit down. "I expected you to be angry. But before you flip out, let me tell you what I need to say."

She told me that she was the one who had cancer, not Dad. When I was about two, she was diagnosed with breast cancer. After a few years of chemotherapy they cured the disease, but in the meantime they cut off both of her breasts.

"I was only twenty. That's too young to lose your breasts. God, I had only gotten them a few years earlier. So when they removed the binding after the operation, I took one look at myself and vowed to never look at myself again. It messed with my mind. I didn't think I would ever grow up and be a woman. And your dad needed a woman. So I took you and we ran away to Vancouver. I told him not to follow us, and I told you that he was dead. He was in some trouble of his own at that time, so I didn't hear from him. But I was always afraid someone would find us, so I shut the curtains and hid out in the apartment—you know that part of the story. I threatened Aunt Lonnie that if she told anyone where we were, I'd run away from her too.

"I knew I wouldn't be able to keep up the lies forever, but I was terrified to tell you the truth. There just never was a good time to admit I was lying. Until this summer, when Aunt Lonnie made a threat of her own. She told me to get to the doctor, get well, and get it together or she would blow the whistle on the whole thing. Your dad had been calling her, and she said she wasn't going to lie for me anymore."

"Dad's not dead?" I didn't know if it was a question or a statement. So I said it again. "Dad's not dead." Either way it sounded like a dream. Then I said, "Dad's alive? Dad's alive," and I started laughing, so hard I was verging on hysterical—like when I was up the mountain.

Mom stopped pacing and sat on my lap. She stroked my hair like I was a little kid and then put my head on her shoulder.

"I'm so sorry, Jona."

I exploded with tears and snot, and Mom took her shawl and wiped my face.

"I'm not sorry," I sputtered. "I have a dad." Jesus, the words sounded like I actually had a dad. "Is this for real?"

"It is. Your dad, Timothy James, is not dead. He's very much alive."

Timothy James. He had a name. I wanted to see his face. And I had a million questions I needed answered. I barely knew where to start. "Timothy James. What's he like?"

"If you want to know what your dad's like, just look in the mirror. You look like him, you're smart like him, and you're a musician like him. So, Jona, I have been learning recently that you are not mine to keep. Even if I wanted to. And I couldn't go on living in fear that he would show up."

"So I'm going to meet my dad for the first time in forever, and I'm a thief."

"I thought you said you didn't steal the ring."

"Seriously, Mom, are you that literal?" I laughed. And we started giggling again, half out of control.

Vik

"Did you tell him?" Bert's voice came from the living room as soon as I opened the door.

"Yeah, I told him." I felt like I was getting buried alive, one shovelful at a time. I stopped in the hall by the living room. "I told him every little detail of the day. What I ate for breakfast, when I went to the bathroom and how long I spent in there. I told him that Linc didn't go to the bathroom and that Jona spent longer in the bathroom than I thought was usual and that, no, I didn't know what he was doing in there."

"Don't sass me, Victoria."

Why not? If I didn't have the guts to tell the truth, the least I could do was give Bert a hard time. "'Cause you know what?" I said. "I don't ask people what they do in the bathroom."

"You think this is funny?"

Nothing was funny, especially Bert. But he was too drunk to get up and fight back, and chances were he wouldn't remember in the morning, so what did I care if I pissed him off?

"You sure as hell better not have tried to cover your scummy little friends' asses."

"I said whatever the hell I wanted to say."

He swung his arms and tried to sit up. "Don't use that language with me, girl." He couldn't get out of the recliner, so he slumped back into the chair, feet in the air. Dell was curled around a coffee cup on the sofa, on the other side of the end table, staring at the TV.

"I'm talking to you." Bert made one last effort to pick a fight with me as I was walking down the hall.

I stopped at my bedroom door.

Leave him alone, I told myself. *He's too drunk to matter.* I wanted to yell at him, though, to tell him that he was an asshole and that he should shut the hell up about the ring. It wasn't even his.

But I was too tired to bother. I shut the door, flopped on my bed, and rolled up in my comforter. I listened to the reassuring rhythm of the foghorn droning in the distance and let the sound drown out the rattling of Bert's voice from the living room.

After a few minutes the house was silent.

Linc to Vik: `Vik, you okay?`

Vik to Linc: `No, you?`

Linc to Vik: `Sorry for all this`

Vik to Linc: `Don't be sorry. It's not your fault`

Linc to Vik: `It's not your fault either`

Yes, it was. I just didn't know what to do about it. If I was going to tell Linc, this wasn't a topic for texts. I needed to see him face to face.

But every time I was about to tell someone the truth, I failed. The trouble was, I was stupid for taking the damn ring out in the first place, and now I was too embarrassed to tell the truth. But knowing the reason wasn't going to help me figure out how to tell Linc what I'd done.

If only I could find the ring. Maybe that would make everything go away, and I wouldn't have to explain anything. How could I find it, though? It could be anywhere from our backyard to TJ's.

Linc to Vik: `I love u`

I loved him right back. Still, I couldn't bring myself to write the words.

Linc to Vik: `See u in the morning`

Vik to Linc: `Okay`

Linc to Vik: `text me when you wake up`

Vik to Linc: 😐

I turned out my bedroom light and stared at the shadows cast on the ceiling by the back porch light. They made me think that I didn't need to wait until the morning. Maybe I could head outside and look for the ring now. But I was exhausted, and before I had time to make a plan, I fell asleep.

1:00 a.m. I don't know what I had been dreaming about, but when I woke up I had one thing in mind—find the ring. Dell had left the porch light on, so I got up and looked into the backyard. It was too dark to see anything, but I thought Bert's hunting flashlight would brighten up the backyard like a football field.

When I went into the hall to the bathroom, I noticed the kitchen light was on as well. Dell was hunched over the table, cradling a teacup.

"How come you're up?" I asked her.

"Bert's snoring. I just want to put a sock in it."

"I can imagine. Or more."

She took a sip and said, "You know, Vik, ever since that damn ring came in the mail, it's been like a curse."

I knew exactly what she meant.

"I loved it and hated it at the same time. Bert was so mad that the ring was all we got out of Mother's estate, but then all he could think about was how rich it would make him if he sold it. And then he was too damn scared to sell it, just in case he could get a few more dollars if he waited."

"It's not even Bert's ring."

"That's just it. I hated the way he thought he owned it. Now it's gone." She sighed. "Maybe we're better off." She took a long drink and stared into her cup. "Maybe now we can be like we used to be. Poor people. I don't think Bert would be any good at being rich. And I didn't like it when I was young, so I don't think I'll miss the ring very much."

Although what she said sounded strange at first, when I thought about it, it made sense—in a twisted kind of way. "I hear you."

I went over to her and hugged her shoulders. She leaned her head into my arms, and for a few seconds I remembered her hugging me when I was a little kid. I wondered when I had stopped calling her Mom—or if I ever did call her that. I wondered if we were ever like a real family. But as hard as I tried, I couldn't remember a day when Bert acted like a father.

"I have to go to the bathroom and get back to bed," I told her, though part of me wanted to stay and talk.

"Me too," she said.

I bent down and kissed her cheek. "I hope you can sleep."

"Yeah. You too."

In bed, I couldn't get Dell's description of the ring as a curse out of my head. She was right. Ever since I picked up the ring, my life had gone from bad to worse. And the weird thing was that I didn't even like the ring. Its gaudiness made me cringe.

Maybe, if Dell thought we'd be happier without it, I shouldn't bother looking for the ring after all.

3:00 a.m. I woke up with dream images floating in my mind. Jona looking cute, smart, sexy. I wanted him. It was dark and eerie, though, and I wondered if he was part of the curse.

Maybe the ring is just a diversion, I thought. *Maybe it's Jona who has messed up your life. He's the curse if anything is. And Jona will mess your life up worse, ring or no ring, if you don't do something about it. Maybe the ring is a blessing, a way to get Jona out of your life.*

Stop it, Vik, I said to myself. *This is just nighttime talk. You don't even believe in stuff like curses and blessings.*

Self-talk wasn't helping me this time. I couldn't stop obsessing about Jona and Linc. Jona might have been able to fool Linc, but he couldn't fool me. Everyone knows that guys can't just be friends with hot girls who are after them. So guys can't just be friends with hot guys who are after them, either.

And what if Bert and Dell were right, and Jona snatched Linc right out from under my nose? I started to shake. I couldn't live without Linc. And to make it worse, I would never be able to live with Bert and Dell constantly reminding me that they had been right.

Dell was right about one thing, though. Being rich wasn't going to solve my problems.

I started to like the idea of not looking for the ring and never finding it. I wouldn't have to lie. I would just have to not tell the truth. Up until now, that had been incredibly easy. The new plan would solve a whole lot of other problems as well. Bert wouldn't get Dell's ring. Jona would be out of the way while he paid for his crime, even if he wasn't paying for exactly the right crime. And Linc and I would be back to normal. The added benefit to my new plan was that I wouldn't have the dreaded embarrassment of admitting it was my fault and revealing how unbelievably pathetic I had been.

The truth had taken so long to come out, it was now almost impossible to tell anyone. *So what,* I said to myself. *There are a million secrets out there that have never been told. Who says you have to tell the truth?*

I tried to think through the plan and make sure I wasn't overlooking anything that would prevent it from working. But I was tired and it was late and the only thing I could decide was that I would leave things alone and let what happened happen. Jona would have to take care of himself. Frankly, I was fed up with thinking about him. Maybe no plan was the best plan of all.

But as I was falling asleep, I started to worry. *Be careful, Vik,* I reminded myself. *Don't start telling lies. There's a difference between not telling the truth and telling an outright lie.*

4:50 a.m. I woke up to the sound of my heart beating so hard I thought it might explode. My forehead was sweaty, as if I had been running in my sleep. I sat up and turned on my bedside lamp.

I hated the plan. I was already tired of the drama. I couldn't imagine spending the rest of my life with it on my conscience. Like it or not, I had to find the ring and settle the problem. I swung my feet over the side of the bed.

I had two hours, at least, before Bert and Dell woke up. I could find Bert's hunting flashlight and tiptoe through the long grass, making sure to follow the path I took earlier. I would search in the cave. How hard could it be?

But what if the neighbours wake up and wonder what the hell is going on in our backyard?

Take the risk, I told myself. *Just do it.*

I pulled on a T-shirt, sweater, and jeans, and stuffed my feet into my running shoes. In the hall, I was surprised to see a light. Dell was standing at the kitchen door. She was wearing her housecoat, which made it stunningly obvious that I needed to find a quick excuse why I was fully dressed. She motioned with her head toward the kitchen.

"What are you doing up?" she whispered.

"I can't sleep."

"You've got your clothes on."

"I got fed up with pretending to sleep."

She nodded as if it made sense.

"If only Jona would bring the ring back," she said.

"God, Dell, what's with the 180-degree turnaround?"

"I got to thinking a little more about it, and I decided that I'm taking the ring back. If I can get it back, I mean."

"What do you mean, take it back?"

"It's mine, not Bert's. And maybe this fiasco has been a good thing. With the help of the cops, and you, if I could just get the ring back, Bert will have to drop the whole thing. I'll take control of what happens to the ring from then on."

I'd like to see that, Dell taking charge. The thought had hardly formed when I gasped. *Oh. My. God! Dell doesn't know it, but she has just solved my problem.*

"I don't think Jona had time to sell it earlier," she continued. "But they've probably let him out already, and someone needs to talk sense into him quickly, before he has time to get rid of it. Someone needs to tell him that I'm willing to drop the whole thing if he would just return the ring." She looked at me as if I was that someone.

"Yeah. Maybe," I said noncommittally. Was there a downside to Jona returning the ring? If there was, I couldn't think of it.

"Do you want to come to the Brig for Sunday brunch this morning?" Dell asked me.

"Me? To the Brig?" I was shocked. Ever since Bert decided I was old enough to stay home by myself, the two of them had been going to the Brig every Sunday without me. "As if Bert's going to want me there."

"It's not about Bert. I want you to come."

Much as I liked the idea of Dell and me telling Bert that I was coming along, I finally had a plan that would work. But it meant finding the ring sooner rather than later. While they were out, in fact.

"I'd like to come with you." I could hardly believe I said that and meant it, but I did. "But Linc's going to phone this morning, and I want to talk to him. It's been a rough day or two."

"Next week then," she said, and I nodded.

"Sure, maybe. Now we need to go back to bed."

Back in my room, I planned everything. I had to find the ring and put it in the jewellery box. Then I had to arrange for Jona to come to the house and give him enough time by himself to make it look like he could have returned the ring. After that, I could just let everything unfold. In a few days the whole thing would be forgotten.

Simple. And the best part was that Jona would be off the

hook and I wouldn't have to live for the rest of my life with the guilt of making him pay for something he didn't do. No one could charge him with stealing the ring if it was sitting in the jewellery box. He might not have been my favourite person at the moment, but I didn't like the thought of him going to jail for something he didn't do. It would be just like the thing I read on the Internet about finding a win-win solution for everyone. Finally, after trying to find a way out of this disaster, it felt like I had stumbled on the right answer. From what I could see, with this plan, it *was* a win-win. No one would get hurt.

9.25 a.m. I rolled over and looked outside. White clouds raced across the blue sky, and the treetops were bending in the wind. The sound of seagulls screaming made me think another storm was coming. I thought of each step of the plan and decided that as long as I found the ring, it would go off without a hitch.

I lay back down and listened to Bert and Dell in the hall. I didn't move for a few more minutes, until I heard the front door close and the car engine start.

The plan might not solve all my problems, but I was thinking that Dell had the right idea—if I could just get this disaster behind me, I would take control of my life and things would be different, better, from now on.

I picked up my cell. Five messages.

Linc to Vik: r u awake?

Linc to Vik: can I come over?

Linc to Vik: yesterday was a bitch let's make today better

Linc to Vik: I love you

Linc to Vik: call me
Vik to Linc: just woke up, call in a little while

Linc

"Linc, you awake?" Mom called up the stairs.

I am now, I said to myself. *But I wish I wasn't.*

I rolled over and looked at the clock. Nine-fifteen.

Linc to Vik: `r u awake?`

Two, three, four texts later and still no answer.

When I saw Jona sitting at the kitchen table, nursing a coffee, I had the urge to give him a hug.

"It's good to see you, bro," I said awkwardly, resisting the urge.

He stood up and grabbed me and slapped me on the back a couple of times. I glanced around the room to make sure Ruby or Billy hadn't shown up already and seen him do it.

"Not as good as it feels to see you," he said, then sat down and took a drink. "When I got up, Mom had gone to work already—two shifts back to back—so I thought I'd pull a Ruby and just drop in."

Mom put a plate of pancakes in front of him. "Want some?" she asked me.

"Yeah. Does that mean I have to watch him eat while I wait?"

She put the butter and syrup on the table and tossed a pile of cutlery in the middle. "You could have come when I called you."

I sat down beside Jona and got the awkward feeling that everyone was probably talking about us. And what if Jona did like me? I mean *really* liked me? I didn't even want to think about whether or not he wanted me. I tried to settle my mind by thinking about some of the things Mom would say: *Go with your instincts. Eat, sleep, run away from animals that will kill you. Fight when you have to. Don't drive too fast. Play soccer. And love your woman.* It made me feel better for a few seconds, and then I worried about where Jona fit in.

"I thought yesterday was gonna be a song," he said. "It turned out to be a whole fucking concert." He put a forkful of pancake, dripping with syrup, into my mouth. "Sorry, bro, to be eating in front of you like this."

"No doubt," I said and wondered about the way he cupped his other hand under my chin. Maybe Ruby was right. I hadn't realized what we looked like together. "How was your mom when you told her?"

He laughed. "That was several songs right there. But the bottom line is that I didn't know shit about myself until last night."

"Tell us more," I said.

"The short version of a very long story is that I am still Jona Prince. Other than that, everything has changed."

He told us that it was his mom who'd had cancer, not his dad. His dad wasn't dead. He was a pilot, flying airliners across the country. The story sounded like something written for Hollywood.

When he was finished, I said, "You're joking."

"No joke, my friend." And he started to sob.

"Sorry, man. What a lame-ass thing to say."

"No worries. I'm not crying 'cause I'm sad. Just a little overwhelmed." He laughed. "A lot overwhelmed."

"I could smell the pancakes from next door," Ruby said as

she walked in. Then "Sorry, man," and she put her arm around Jona.

"It's okay." He wiped his nose on a napkin. "I can explain."

When he was telling Ruby the part about his dad, I looked at Mom. Her eyes were filled with tears, and I could feel the same thing happening to me. I knew we were both wishing it had all been a lie, and that one night over a can of Pepsi she could tell me the truth and, voila, Dad would turn up.

"All of this brings up some complications," he said, pulling himself together. He gulped down the rest of his milk. "I'm supposed to go to Ontario to see my grandma, who doesn't have long to live, and visit my dad. But now I'm a thief, I'm sort of worried about the reunion."

I almost gagged. "You're a thief?"

"No! I mean, everyone *thinks* I'm a thief, and how's that going to be for my dad? 'Oh, meet your son Jona. He's going to spend the next five years in jail.'"

"You're not going to spend one more day in jail," Ruby said. "Somehow something is going to happen to make the truth turn up."

"I wish I could be as positive as you are," he said. "That Hopper dude has got it in for me, big time. That man sweats hate out of his pores. If he's in charge of the case, then I'm pretty sure this is going to be a 'guilty until proven innocent' situation."

"We'll find a way to prove you are innocent," Ruby said in her usual positive way.

"How can I prove I didn't do something? All I can say is that I just didn't do it. And look at me," he said, pointing to himself. "It feels like I'm guilty just because I look…" He stopped and threw his hands up in the air.

"I hate to rain on your legal defence's parade," I said to Ruby. "But if you prove Jona is innocent, they are going to swing around and start looking right in my direction."

"Yeah, you're right," Jona agreed. "It sounded like Hopper was trying to get me to implicate you."

"They want one of us," I said. "The only thing I have going for me is that Vik is my alibi. I just wish I could get a hold of her."

I told Ruby and Jona the questions Firth was asking, and Ruby said, "That's stupid. We'll just have to make both of you innocent."

"God, I hate things I don't understand," Mom said. "I want to know who the hell took the ring."

"I thought you said we had to be patient," I said. "And that the truth would unfold."

Vik

When I heard the car pull out of the driveway, I stuck my head out my bedroom door and yelled, "Dell, are you home?"

The house was empty. In the hall, I called again. "Dell, are you home?"

I stood at the front window to check for the car. It was gone.

This was the time I had been waiting for. But what if I couldn't find the ring? I breathed in, one two three four, and out, one two three four. *Then it'll be Plan B,* I told myself. *Tell Linc and get a metal detector.*

I went out the back door onto the porch. The early morning wind had blown the clouds away, and the seagulls with them. The air was calm, and all was quiet, except for the sound of a few Sunday-morning cars on the road. The grass was wet, but I could still see my footprints in shadows across the backyard. I stepped off the porch and tried to place each foot in the same impressions I had made the day before. I examined the area around each step for any sign of a disturbance: a blade of grass bent differently than the rest; a glimpse of anything that looked like metal or glass. I cast my eyes out into the largest circumference that I could see without stepping off my original path. I didn't want to think of the possibility that the ring might have flown off my finger while I was running and was lying in the long grass, somewhere way off course, too far for me to see. It felt as if my heart had crept up my throat and was blocking my windpipe. I swallowed hard to get enough air.

My feet were soaking and cold when I reached the hedgerow under the maple tree, with its tangle of bushes and vines. *My God, how can I find anything in that?* I closed my eyes and swallowed my sobs.

My plan had seemed easy when I was in bed. Now the ring seemed so small, and the backyard so huge. I thought, *Maybe this is when people would say a prayer.* But I didn't know what to say. *If there is a God,* I thought, *he or she would not have time to worry about little things like my missing ring. How could such a tiny thing become such an enormous problem?*

I crouched down and tried to sneak through the same opening I had made the previous day. As I moved, I delicately shuffled through the growth and debris near the ground. I moved slowly, and each time I touched something and did not find the ring, another wave of panic threatened to close my airway altogether. To make matters worse, each time I moved, the leaves overhead dumped what felt like buckets of cold water on my head and down my back.

When I reached my cave, I collapsed on the moss and buried my face in my knees. Where could it be? The loud chirping of a squirrel interrupted the quiet. I looked up. There wasn't one squirrel, but two or three or four of them sitting on the branches of an oak tree. Their chirping sounded like they were mocking me.

Hah, they were saying. *Just try and find the ring now.*

Oh my God, is it possible? Could a squirrel have picked up the ring? And dropped it? Anywhere?

I lowered my head and forced myself to look at the ground

around where I had been sitting. The round indentation of my bum and scuff marks from my feet were still pressed into the soft moss. I moved toward what would have been my left side, the hand that wore the ring. On my hands and knees, I bent so low my nose almost touched the ground.

My eyes filled with tears. There was no trace of the ring. "Oh, no." I started to cry. "Please, please, I cannot go back into the house without it."

I sat on the wet moss, looked back through the opening in the hedgerow, and caught a glimpse of something in a pile of soggy maple leaves. Something metallic. I rolled up onto my knees and placed my hands carefully near the wet leaves so I didn't disturb anything. I held my breath, leaned down, and looked, as if I were peering through a microscope, and saw the tip of the tiny gold band.

I reached in and picked it up. I stared at the emerald and diamonds and then at the pile of leaves and thought, *What if I had stepped on it, or kicked it, or moved the leaves even slightly? The ring would have disappeared.* I felt like I had just avoided a terrible traffic accident; by pure luck I had gotten out with my life.

I put the ring in the palm of my hand and wrapped my fingers around it. I opened them and peeked to make sure it was still there. I closed my fingers. I climbed back through the hedgerow and walked along the path across the lawn. I stopped halfway and opened my fingers. The ring was still in my palm. I stopped again when I reached the porch. The ring had safely made it to the house.

With one hand and a fist, I took off my soaking coat and shoes and left them outside the door.

I opened the door to Dell and Bert's room and shut it behind me. The jewellery box was still open on the dresser. I folded the green velvet cloth around the ring and placed it on top of the newspaper clipping.

I opened the blanket box, dug into the centre of the linens, and nestled the jewellery box back where I had found it. I deliberately left the linens in a messy pile so it looked like a boy had been in a hurry. I closed the box and locked it, then put the key in the dresser drawer. Having second thoughts, I took the key out of the drawer, unlocked the box, and left the key on top of the dresser to give another hint that Jona was rushing. I paused and thought again. It looked too obvious—like it had been planted there to give that impression.

God, Vik, I said to myself, *you are acting like a criminal. Like you have done this before.* The thought stunned me. It was one thing to think of a plan; another thing to actually pull it off. *This isn't criminal,* my self-talk continued. *This is simply necessary to get everyone out of trouble. The truth is that when you are backed in a corner, there are very few ways out.*

I grabbed a hand towel from the laundry basket and wiped my fingerprints off the lid of the blanket box.

Fingerprints. Had they checked for prints the day before? I wiped everything I might have touched—the dresser, the door handles, both sides of the door. I wiped the marks from my wet feet off the floor as I backed toward the door. I threw the towel into the basket and repositioned it so it was as it had been when I picked it up. I wrapped my sleeve around my hand to avoid putting prints on the newly cleaned door handles. I took a final look at the room—everything was in place, exactly as it had been. I checked again to be sure that I had left no traces.

I leaned against the wall in the hallway, rehashing the details of the room. There was nothing more I could do but get on with my plan. I checked the time. So far I had used less than thirty minutes. Dell and Bert wouldn't be home for at least another hour and a half.

My fingers vibrated when I texted Linc.

Linc

My cell beeped.

Vik to Linc: `What are u doing?`

Linc to Vik: `nothing`

Vik to Linc: `When are u coming over?`

Linc to Vik: `soon`

Vik to Linc: `Can you bring Jona?`

Why the hell does she want him over at her place? Didn't she want it to be all about her?

Linc to Vik: `Really? Jona? What for?`

Vik to Linc: `I need to apologize`

Linc to Vik: `No u don't`

Vik to Linc: `yes I do...want to do it here`

Linc to Vik: `no way`

I didn't even want him to come with me. I needed to be with Vik, alone, and have the conversation we were going to have before all hell broke out.

Vik to Linc: `Bert and Dell are out – we can get out of here quickly`

Linc to Vik: `not a good idea. But I'll ask him`

Vik to Linc: `thanks see u soon`

"Was that Vik?" Ruby asked. "How is she? What did she say?"

I put my phone down. "I don't get that girl."

"Why? What happened? Is she all right?"

"Yeah, she's all right, I guess. But she wants Jona and me to come over."

"No way," Jona said. He leaned back and laughed as if I was joking. "I won't be going to Vik's place anytime soon. What do they say? Once bitten twice shy?"

"Seriously," I said. Though I totally understood where he was coming from, there was something about Vik's request that made me want to convince him. "She said she needs to apologize."

"For what? What did she do?"

"Probably for her dad."

"That's not her fault. And for real, bro, I'd like to stay a long way from her place and especially her old man."

"He won't be home," I said. "It seems like it's important to her. I promise we'll just rush in and let her do her thing and then rush out again."

"Shit. I really, really don't want to go back there."

I reached over and gave his shoulder a squeeze. "God. Your shoulders are tight! You should relax, man! Maybe if we go over there and hear Vik out, it'll help us both relax."

"Okay, okay. I'll go. But I'm going to keep my eye on the driveway, and if that old bastard drives in, I'll be out of there so fast you won't see me go."

"I'll be right behind you."

Jona

Generally I thought I was a street-savvy sort of guy. Living in East Vancouver gave me a few skills. Like, for instance, number one on that list was that I learned how to stay out of trouble. Other than my stupid decision to get into the car with Arwen, it wasn't like me to walk right in with my eyes open.

When we stopped in Vik's driveway, I thought about Mom's question. *Do you do everything Linc says?* My armpits were clamming up and my saliva was evaporating—two clues that I was getting close to trouble.

"This seems like a really bad idea," I said to Linc. "How about I hang out in the van while you go in and get her?"

"I hear you. But this seems pretty important to Vik. She wants us both to come in so she can do some apology thing."

"Can't she do that at your place? Or in the car?" I felt like I was walking toward a cliff, and Linc was holding my hand so I wasn't afraid. My brain was screaming at me, *God, Jona, listen to your instincts—Bert is dangerous—the house is dangerous—stay away from dangerous things.*

Linc got out of the car. "Come on. It'll only take a few minutes. I promise. Don't sweat it."

Hadn't he said the same thing yesterday?

He walked around the front of the van and opened my

door. "Just this once," he said. He scrunched his face up like a little kid begging for an ice cream cone. "Please." How could I say no?

"Okay. Okay. For crap's sake, let's be fast."

"I hear you." But I could tell that he was thinking about Vik, not me or even himself. I knew when I jumped out of the van that Linc would have been willing to walk right into a snakepit if he thought it would make Vik happy. I admired his commitment, though I was worried that this time he'd tossed better judgment out the window. "But let's just let Vik do her thing. It seems really important to her. Let's trust her on this one."

"Trust?" I almost laughed. "I don't think I trust anyone right now." My eyes darted around, and I half expected Bert to jump out from behind a tree with a baseball bat.

While I followed Linc up the stairs, I realized something I really liked about him. He was there for Vik. She might not think so all the time, but he was willing to put it out there and take a risk for her. I thought about how much I would love someone to do that for me. How much I'd love Linc to feel that way about me.

I was shaking by the time he rang the doorbell.

"Calm down," he said. He put his hand on the small of my back, which did the exact opposite of calming me down.

Vik was smiling when she opened the door. She looked a little bit like the girl I met the first day of school. She threw her hands out to Linc and fell forward into his arms.

"Come on in. Bert and Dell are at the Brig. They'll get home about one, so we don't have much time."

Linc looked perfectly calm. He scooped her up off her feet

and wrapped his arms around her. They looked like a happy couple.

Had everyone forgotten that a ring was missing and that I was the prime suspect? Had they forgotten that Bert had promised to kill me?

"Hey, Jona," she said, and her face tightened up a bit, which I thought was, at least, a small recognition that there was a crisis happening. "Thanks for coming over."

Linc sauntered into the living room behind Vik, as if we had all the time in the world. But I wasn't buying the relaxed thing. Vik needed to do her apologies so I could get out of there.

"I hate this house," she said. "I can't stand another minute here with Dell and Bert."

I thought, *No kidding. I know exactly how you feel.* And that started me thinking that maybe I didn't know how she felt. Did she *really* want us there to make some sort of weird amends for the house and her family?

"I needed you guys to be here in this house so that I could apologize. I am so embarrassed about what happened yesterday. And so embarrassed it was my father and in my house. You should be safe here." Tears welled up in her eyes, and I got the feeling she really meant it. "It was so, so, so wrong. I'm saying sorry now because I want to make it right."

I sort of got her point and thought, *Nice.* And even though she'd started to look like she had a bee up her butt half the time, I remembered why I really liked her, right from the start.

I moved sideways a few steps so I had a full view of the driveway. I calculated the distance from the car to the house, and estimated how much time I would have to run out the back door when Bert's car pulled in. I had nothing to worry about. I would be into the neighbour's yard before he had time to open the front door.

"Thanks, babe. We're okay. We're going to find a way out of this."

Then I got thinking that was fine for him to say. But weren't we missing the real issue? An heirloom was missing, he was standing there with his alibi, and I was the prime suspect.

"Yeah," I said, trying to follow Linc's lead and politely skirt the issue. "Thanks, Vik, for this. Yesterday was a bad day for everyone, but you don't need to apologize. It wasn't your fault. Though I sure as hell hope something good shows up today."

"It will. I know it will." She was almost exuberant. What the hell had happened to her? She was like a completely different person.

Vik gave Linc a long, wet kiss. Her hands moved down over his ass, and she squirmed closer to him until they had full body contact.

Looking for something to do with my eyes, I checked the driveway for any sign of Bert.

"Come in here." She stood on her tiptoes and whispered in his ear, then nodded her chin toward the kitchen. "Just for one minute." She turned to me and asked, "Do you mind, Jona? I just want a couple of minutes with Linc, alone."

God, if I'd ever needed convincing that girls were way too complicated, I didn't need it anymore.

"Yeah, yeah," I said, thinking it would be a good thing if they took their business into the other room. "I'll wait here."

I stood a few steps behind the curtains, out of sight from the driveway but with a clear view of it right out to the road. I recalculated my escape plan. It wasn't a very big house. Keeping an eye on the driveway, I glanced around the room. A plaque with the motto *Look on the bright side* caught my eye. *Yeah, right,* I thought.

Vik

Linc followed me into the kitchen, and we stood by the window, looking out over the backyard. He frowned when he saw my footprints. The way the light hit the grass, they looked like giant paving stones.

Without thinking, I took his hand and led him out onto the back porch. "I did the weirdest thing this morning," I told him. "I used to go out there when I was a kid." I pointed in the direction of the cave. "When I ran away from Bert, I'd crawl through the hedgerow. I thought it was such a long way from the house, and now it looks so close."

He looked confused.

"Bert wouldn't follow me, so I thought I was safe."

He hugged me. "It must be hell living with him. I'm sorry I couldn't protect you yesterday."

"Please don't say you're sorry." I paused and gathered my nerve. "There's a little clearing inside, and I went out there and sat on the moss. I got soaking wet. But that's when I knew I had to apologize."

How was I going to keep the secret from Linc? Would I have to start making up little lies? And then would I have to remember all the little lies that I had told?

"Thanks for telling me about that, Vik."

Telling half the truth was so easy, and he believed me.

He held me close, but I felt dirty, like my skin was covered in grime and I needed a shower. I was trembling inside, but this time it wasn't Bert I was afraid of. I was afraid of the person I had become. Was I really willing to tell an outright lie? Was I willing to let everyone blame Jona and then deliberately frame him so I could get away scot-free? What happened to the girl I used to be, who was committed to cleaning the streams and making the world a better place?

When we pulled out of the driveway, Jona said, "Phew. I can breathe now. That was fucking scary."

"I told you, bro," Linc said. "It all turned out okay."

"Except for one little detail. It hasn't turned out yet. I'm still on the hook for a missing ring that I did not steal."

I thought, *Not anymore. I just made sure of that.*

I looked at Linc. He would hate me if he knew. All of a sudden my little scheme didn't look so good. I wouldn't be able to keep the truth from him for a week, never mind forever.

My cell rang as we crossed the bridge. "It's Dell," I told Linc. "What do you think she wants?"

"I don't know. Answer it."

I looked at the time. She couldn't possibly be home. I pressed *Talk*. "What?"

"The cops are on their way to the house. They need to take some fingerprints. Can you believe it? They didn't take any yesterday."

"I'm not home." I wondered if they could get my fingerprints off the cloth. "I'm on my way over to Linc's."

"Bert's not going to be happy about that."

"I'm not trying to make Bert happy."

"We're going home to meet them. But I want you there as well."

I should have been relieved. The whole thing would be settled in a matter of hours. The cops would find the ring, there would be no fingerprints, Linc and I would testify that Jona had plenty of time to replace the ring. Case closed. But I couldn't go home. I wasn't sure I'd ever be able to go home, case closed or not. I would never be able to live with Bert reminding me that he was right about my friends.

"I'll be at Linc's. Call me if you need me."

"Of course they won't find my fingerprints in the room," Jona said when I hung up and repeated what Dell had said. "I didn't steal the ring."

"They never took any prints yesterday," I said.

"They can take all the prints of these babies they want." He held his hands up next to Linc and me and wiggled his fingers around like he was doing an old-lady wave. "They won't find them in that bedroom."

He was right. What he didn't know was that they wouldn't find any fingerprints at all. But they would just think he had erased them, like I did.

"I wish we didn't have to talk about it anymore," I said.

"Me too," Linc said, and he turned up the radio.

"I agree with both of you. I wish that I didn't have to think about it either. But as it turns out, I am very bad at ignoring the fact that I've been charged with stealing something I didn't steal, and the cops are out this morning looking for evidence to nail me."

If only I could fast-forward time. If it could be tomorrow, or a week from now, this would be in the past. Bert would have no proof against Jona. Dell would be in control of the ring. Everyone would have forgotten about the whole thing. And Linc and I would be back to normal. *Yeah, right, Vik,* I said to myself. *None of that is going to happen, in spite of your scheme.*

Ruby met us on the porch. She rushed down the stairs and opened the van door on my side.

"Vik, I'm so glad you're here, girl." She grabbed me as I slid off the seat and gave me a hug. "Sandy's got some breakfast inside. Come on."

The smell of pancakes and coffee reminded me that I was hungry. When Sandy served me a plate of pancakes with strawberries and bananas, I put my head down and ate. I half listened to Ruby telling Jona how she intended to get everyone together to brainstorm ways to defend him. But it wasn't right. Nothing was right. Even if the cops believed that Jona returned the ring, it wasn't right. Even if Dell convinced Bert to leave it alone, it still wasn't right. Even if Linc believed every lie I told, and if I finally believed the lies myself, it was all completely wrong.

I lifted my head and saw Dell coming into the kitchen. I took a gulp of air, thinking, *This is it. They've found the ring and I'm going to have to look surprised.* Maybe I would even have to look at Jona and say something like "Did you put it back?" Would I need to cry and look hurt, or would it be better if I feigned anger?

"I want you to come home with me," Dell said, and I realized she hadn't been home yet. "I dropped Bert at home and came to get you. I need you, Vik. I don't want to deal with Bert anymore. Ring or no ring."

Linc pulled out a chair. "Sit down," he said to her.

Sandy and Ruby were sitting across the table from me, and

Linc was beside me. Dell and Jona sat at each end. I looked around and realized that everyone I needed to talk to was at the table.

"Just a minute," I said. "Maybe we can all go with you."

Everyone heard what I said, but no one could have possibly understood why I said it. I tried to think of the perfect words to explain. My eyes filled with tears.

"I just need to say something first." I started to cry.

Linc put his arm around me. Sandy and Ruby reached across the table to hold my hands.

Linc said, "We understand, Vik. It's not your fault."

I pushed him away and said, "Yes, it is." Then I got up and went into the bathroom and blew my nose. I looked in the mirror. I took a deep breath and said to myself, *It's time, Vik, for you to tell the truth.*

They all looked confused when I returned. "It is my fault. It's all my fault, and I'm sorry."

Then I told them the whole story, from start to finish. I didn't leave anything out or put anything in.

"I don't expect you all to forgive me," I said when I reached the end. "But I have to forgive myself. I am at least happy to know that I couldn't go through with it. As much as I was jealous and angry and worried and hurt and afraid, I couldn't lie and hurt someone else."

Linc

Everyone got in the van, and we drove over to Vik's house. Dell opened the front door and then stepped aside and motioned for me to go in first. I guess there's truth in the saying "There's strength in numbers," because I wasn't afraid.

Bert was sitting in his recliner with his feet up, watching football on TV. When he saw me, he kicked the footrest and sat up straight.

"What the hell are you…?" he said and then watched as the others came in. Vik was next, then Sandy, Ruby, and Jona, and Dell shut the door behind everyone.

Vik stepped in front of me. "We're here to let you know that Dell's ring is back in the jewellery box. I put it there this morning after I found it out in the backyard."

Bert didn't move. He looked like he was trying to understand but couldn't.

"I also want to say that I'm going to pack a suitcase and move out. I'll be staying at Ruby's house for a while, until I can figure out a permanent place. I can't do this pretend-family thing we've got going on here."

Bert took a gulp of beer and opened his mouth as if he was going to start in on her, but then he closed it again.

"We'll be checking up on Dell," Mom said. "She's not sure

what she's going to do with her ring, but we're going to make sure she's safe whatever happens."

"It's her ring, Bert," Vik said.

"But, but..." Bert pulled himself to the edge of the chair. "What the hell do you mean?"

"I said what I mean," Vik said. I was close enough to feel her body trembling, but on the surface she looked like she had everything under control. "If you want the details, you can ask me sometime. If I feel like it, I'll tell you."

Like an old fighter with one more round in him, Bert looked at Jona. "The cops are on their way, boy. You won't get away with this. Getting my daughter to do your dirty work."

"Never mind with your bullshit," Vik said. "This is the first clean work I've done for a while. The cops will only need to apologize to Jona for accusing him of doing something he didn't do."

At first I had been angry with Vik for putting Jona and me through the wringer. But when she went down the hall to pack her stuff, I realized I hadn't understood what she had lived with. I followed her into her room and said, "Don't tell me not to say I'm sorry, because I am. And just one more thing: I love you. Jona is my friend, and I hope he can be your friend as well. You are not going to lose me, babe, to a boy."

Jona

Logically, it all made sense. Vik didn't know what the hell to do about the ring, so she didn't do anything. She let the whole crazy thing unfold into chaos, and everyone was looking in the wrong direction for the culprit. Except Mom. I remembered the thing she had said, that maybe Vik and Linc were framing me. Brilliant. But logic wasn't very helpful when you wanted to understand people, because most of the time people weren't logical. For instance, there was nothing logical about the disaster people had made of the mountain, or how amazing I felt when I helped plant a few bags of seedlings. There wasn't anything logical about how attracted I was to Linc or how much he loved Vik.

While Vik was packing, Hopper and Mainwaring drove up. Dell went outside and talked to them. I stood close to the door so I could hear what they were saying, but I could only catch a few words. She said something about it being her ring and that there had been a big mistake. The cops nodded and shook her hand. I heard Hopper say, "Call if you need us." And Dell said, "I'm so sorry for wasting your time."

When they left, she came back inside and went straight into her room. She returned with a little green velvet bundle. We all peered into her hands as she untied the ribbon and pulled the covering back.

"Holy," Ruby said when she saw the humongous ring. Her hand shot toward it, but just as quickly pulled back again.

"Go ahead," Dell said. "Pick it up and put it on. It doesn't bite."

I guess you could say it was beautiful, but other than the Academy Awards, I didn't know when you would wear it. On Ruby's finger it looked like it was on steroids.

Bert pushed his butt back into his chair and curled around his beer. He looked like a pitiful old man. But there was nothing logical about him, either. There was no damn way I was going to trust him. I was pretty sure he could become a raging lunatic without a moment's notice.

While the others hovered around the ring, I stepped outside and sat on the front stairs. Two bald eagles soared overhead, dipping down into the bay on the other side of the trees. After a minute, one of them flew past with a salmon locked in its talons. The fish looked about half the size of the eagle and was flapping for its life. The eagle flew off as if the fish wasn't even there.

I pulled out my pen and notepad. Words started showing up without any thought:

He's my Mohawk man
A wild word warrior strumming revolution
Beating convolution,
Coming up with the solution on his eagle guitar
He's making Oka music with his blood and bones
and supersonic drones
He's clearing the roads to the new world
To the new world coming
My boy, her boy
Paint your masks with the rainbow and flow with my hero

On the back of the bird
Absurd
Soar, explore, and more on the back of the bird

I figured out that stories about lies often end up being stories about the truths that we don't know about each other, and the truths we don't know about ourselves. And that uncovering a lie can uncover a whole lot more than that—it can uncover who we really are.

AKNOWLEDGEMENTS

Many thanks to a team of brilliant editors—Barbara Pulling, Nikki Tate, Audrey McClellan, and Dawn Loewen—as well as designer Frances Hunter, who got behind this project and pulled together to make it happen. You all went beyond the call of duty on this book. So did Sono Nis Press, providing such amazing support. Thanks to Marie Bourque for helping me imagine and describe the police scenes, and to Solara Goldwynn for sharing her knowledge of tree planting and forest recovery. And thanks to Maddy, my granddaughter, and Tex, my patient partner, for your willingness to read and critique this story.